MISSION: LOVE

"Now I see who's been on your mind," my friend Sara said.

My blush must have gone ten times redder.

"It's either Lawrence Kramer, Greg Segura, or Jim Ryba." Sara thought for a moment. "I give up, Allie. Who is it?"

I didn't answer. All I could think about was the fact that Greg was just a few yards away from me, ordering an ice cream cone. Greg—with his cute freckled nose and that gymnast's glide in his walk.

"It's Jim," Sara whispered, snapping me out of my daydream.

I looked at her blankly.

"Ah-hah!" she cried. "I knew it!"

"No, Sara. You're wrong—" I stopped myself. Why not let her think I was interested in Jim? At least for now.

Bantam Sweet Dreams Romances
Ask your bookseller for the books you have missed.

Mission: LOVE

Kathryn Makris

BANTAM BOOKS
TORONTO · NEW YORK · LONDON · SYDNEY · AUCKLAND

RL 5, age 11 and up

MISSION: LOVE

A Bantam Book / March 1986

ISBN 0-553-25470-7

Published simultaneously in the United States and Canada

Bantam Books are published by Bantam Books, Inc. Its trademark,
consisting of the words "Bantam Books" and the portrayal of
a rooster, is Registered in U.S. Patent and Trademark Office
and in other countries. Marca Registrada. Bantam Books, Inc.,
666 Fifth Avenue, New York, New York 10103.

PRINTED IN THE UNITED STATES OF AMERICA

O   0 9 8 7 6 5 4 3 2 1

To M.S.M.,
my brother and friend,
to whom I owe (among other things)
the idea for this book

Chapter One

"Hey, Allie! Where're you headed?"

My knees wobbled at the sound of his voice. It was one thing for Greg Segura to turn around and ask to borrow an eraser in history, where I spent most of the period staring at his beautiful auburn hair. It was another thing entirely for him to pick me out of a whole crowd of people in the middle of the hall and start walking with me. I'm not used to boys picking me out of whole crowds of people.

"Oh, I'm going to math class," I answered, trying to keep my voice steady while gazing back into his chocolate brown eyes. One of the terrific things about Greg is that he is one boy I don't have to strain my neck to look up at. At five-foot-two, I have that problem often. Not with Greg. He's just the right height.

"Math, huh," he said. "You must have Landry."

I nodded. "What's your next class?"

"Biology. Upstairs." He hooked a thumb toward the stairwell in front of us. When we got there he stopped, and for a moment we just looked at each other. "Well, I'd better be going," he finally said.

Greg flashed his dynamite smile at me as he took off up the stairs. I was amazed that it didn't make me keel over with joy. Almost, but not quite.

"See you later, Allison Perrin-James," he called, making my whole complicated name sound dignified and important.

I smiled back and kept smiling all the way to math class.

Mine are not the kind of knees that get wobbly over any little thing. They need a good reason. Greg Segura was definitely a good reason. Several times during math class, I caught myself twirling one of my blond curls and staring out the window at the wisteria vines trailing over the walkway. The sun glistened on the purple blossoms, and a soft breeze rustled them. With the deep blue sky overhead, it all added up to a picture-perfect California day. Spring fever, I thought. Maybe that was what I was coming down with.

When the class ended, I made a beeline for the Pit. The Pit is our name for the first-floor girls' bathroom. Aside from me, the only people who call it that are Marion Duvall, Sara Novello, and Nicky Gould. They're my best friends, and the only ones who'd really understand the way I'd been feeling since Greg walked me down the hall. They knew my dating history, which was about as exciting as watching grass grow.

I burst through the swinging door and let out a yell. "Hey, Marion! You in here?" I asked, pushing through the crowd in front of the mirror. "Must be," I said, peeking under a stall door. "I can see your feet."

One of those feet kicked out at me. "You don't have to announce it," she hissed.

At that moment, though, I felt like announcing everything: The earth is round! The sky is blue! Greg Segura talked to me!" But I couldn't because the Pit was filled with too many people who wouldn't understand.

"Hurry up, Marion," I pleaded. "I have to talk to you."

"Leave me alone," she muttered.

"But it's *important*."

Marion didn't answer. All I heard was a kind of muffled little sniffle and then the toilet being flushed. I didn't pressure her after that.

Especially not after I heard her blowing her nose. I realized why Marion was hiding out in the stall. She was crying.

"Marion," I whispered, knocking softly. "Marion, are you OK?"

By then, the crowd around the mirror had thinned out.

"No," she mumbled. "No, I'm not."

With that, she unlocked the door and opened it. As usual, I felt like a pudgy little dwarf beside her. Although I'm about the right weight for my height, everything about me is very round—eyes, cheeks, even my mouth. My mother's favorite word to describe me has always been "cherubic," and whenever she calls me that, I want to scream and hand my "cute button nose" right back to her. Marion, however, is different. At five-foot-nine, she commands any room. With her slender figure and silky dark skin, she looks like an exotic princess.

"What's wrong?" I asked, looking up at her delicate but now puffy features. "Are you sick?"

"Yes, I'm sick." She said it so angrily that her black eyes flashed. "I'm sick of *him*!"

"Of Burke?" I whispered, still in shock that calm, reserved Marion was so upset.

"I don't want to talk about it." She pushed

past me to the mirror and dabbed at her smudged mascara.

Of the four of us, Marion is the one I would have least expected to find falling apart in the bathroom. She is always poised and sophisticated. She has even modeled junior fashions for a fancy department store downtown, and one summer the local chapter of the Black Women of America gave her its Teen Achievement Award for her good grades and hard work in extracurricular activities.

I followed her to the mirror and reached up to put my hand on her shoulder. "What happened?"

"Nothing," she said shakily.

"Marion, we've never kept secrets from each other. Tell me what's wrong. Maybe I can help."

"You can't," she sniffled. "No one can. He's—he's"—she covered her mouth with the tissue so I wouldn't see her lip tremble—"he's *cheating* on me!"

I glanced around to make sure no one was listening. We were alone and probably about to be late for class. But Marion's problem was important.

"Cheating?" I whispered.

She nodded so miserably that I tightened my grip on her shoulder.

"But that's ridiculous," I said softly. "Burke's nuts about you. He would never—"

"Yes, he would!" Marion whirled around to face me.

"Marion, wait a second. How did you get this idea, for heaven's sake?"

She sniffed again, then blew her nose. "I can tell. Just like last time. He's starting to act just the way Richard did when—when—"

"Oh, Marion." I set my free hand on her other shoulder and gave her a little sideways hug. "Don't do this to yourself. Just because you got burned by one no-good creep of a guy doesn't mean it'll happen again."

"I can tell, though," she insisted. "Burke is so distant sometimes, as if he couldn't care less about me."

"Marion, you've been going with Burke Walters for three months. You've been having a great time. At least you always tell us so. And Burke is crazy about you. Everyone knows that. Don't get all bent out of shape because he isn't as super-glued to you as he was in the beginning."

Marion took a deep breath, as if to say she was done with her outburst. Her shoulders straightened, and even with her smudged makeup she looked like her dignified, graceful self again.

Rearranging thé smooth, dark bangs over her forehead, she said, "We'll see. You just watch him this afternoon when we get pizza."

After helping her unsmudge her makeup and pull herself together, I dashed out of the Pit to my next class. At least Marion had gotten her worries off her chest for a while. Eventually, she'd forget all about Richard Pinson's unfaithfulness and start trusting guys again.

Trusting guys. I had certainly never had much trouble doing that. All the guys I had ever dated—a grand total of two—had been as predictable as corn flakes. With Kevin Neville, I spent homecoming night combing through the weeds under the bleachers for classic Coke bottle caps, which he collected. John Mathers, the video game freak, always parked himself in front of people's home computers at parties. It had been a month since I'd been out with either one of them. And it would be at least that much longer before I'd try it again. Someone more interesting, I kept telling myself, was bound to come along. Someone like Greg.

Suddenly that warm, bubbly feeling I'd had earlier returned. Greg Segura was definitely interesting. After a semester of sitting behind him in class, I was *very* interested. I knew I wouldn't mind getting to know more than the back of his head.

What I needed to do was to talk the matter over with my friends. I had never mentioned Greg before because practically all there was to mention was his beautiful reddish-brown hair, the proud way he held his shoulders, and the fact that he had a small button nose like mine. But that afternoon in the Pit hadn't exactly seemed like the right time to mention any of it. Marion didn't need to hear about Greg just then.

Oh, well, I thought, smiling again. Maybe I'd tell her and the rest of the gang about him after school at Pete's Pizza.

As it turned out, though, I didn't get to say a word about Greg there, either. Too many other people were crammed into our booth, and I wasn't about to mention Greg around them.

Burke had squeezed himself in next to Marion, acting as hopelessly devoted to her as always. His dark eyes rarely left her. Just once he looked away to run a comb through his short Afro. I didn't notice anything about him that Marion could possibly get upset over.

"Mmmm. You smell nice," he told her at one point, holding his long arm around her and nuzzling her ear.

Marion smiled her Mona Lisa, unreadable smile and leaned toward him just a little. It seemed to me that she had recovered from her panic attack in the bathroom.

"We gave her that perfume for Christmas," Nicky piped up. Her blue eyes, set off by the fiery red of her long, wavy hair, sparkled mischievously. "It's called Temptation."

Dennis Conroy whistled. "Temptation. Wow! Are you wearing it, too?" He leaned over to sniff at Nicky's hair, but she shoved him away and shot a warning glance at Bob Lopez. They were a couple of her latest admirers. Nicky always had at least two or three guys hovering around her.

"Nicky doesn't *need* to wear Temptation," I teased.

"Oh?" Marion raised her eyebrows. "And I suppose I do?"

Sara covered her mouth with her hand and snickered. It made her look like the little brown mouse she always accused herself of resembling.

"You've got to admit," I answered Marion, "if you were being cast in a movie, don't you think they'd have you play the cool, sophisticate instead of the temptress?"

She nodded. "I suppose."

"Hey," Dennis said. "Talk about movies, has anyone seen that new James Bond flick?"

"I did," I answered.

"Allie sees *every* James Bond movie," Nicky said. "As soon as it comes out."

"And," Marion added, "she's read practically every spy and detective novel there is."

Marion wasn't kidding. I have a thing for spy stories. It's fun to try to uncover secrets. On the other hand, though, I'm very good at keeping them.

After another round of sodas, Burke had to leave for his job at the grocery store, and Nicky started to shoo away her admirers.

"OK, guys," she told Dennis and Bob. "It's time for some private talk here."

Good, I thought. I'd finally get a chance to tell them about Greg.

"Fine with me," Bob said, resting his chin on a fist.

"Yeah," Dennis assured us. "We'll be private."

"You know what I mean," Nicky said, giving Bob a shove. "Out! We girls need to be *alone.*"

"Oh, all right," Dennis said, giving in and getting out of the booth. "But you'll be at lunch tomorrow, won't you?"

"Of *course* I'll be at lunch." Nicky aimed her famous eye roll at them. "Bye."

Dennis clicked his heels and saluted, and Bob bowed on his way out.

"Talk about wrapped," I muttered.

"Around your little finger," Sara added, staring at Nicky in absolute awe.

"Oh, cut it out," Nicky said, laughing. "You know they're just clowning around."

"In that case, you've got a whole circus full of clowns after you," Marion pointed out.

Nicky shrugged. Through a mouthful of ice, she said, "Not my fault."

"I could use such problems," Sara said. A wave of pretty chestnut hair fell over her cheek.

Nicky, crunching on her ice, tried to speak. "I toll you I'd fiss you up whiff shumbuddy."

"You what?" Sara asked as she squinted through her glasses at Nicky.

I had been trying to think up the most exciting way to tell them about Greg, but I stopped to translate for Sara. "She said she'd fix you up with somebody."

It was Sara's turn to roll her eyes. "I don't *want* you to fix me up with anyone, Nicky."

"It's because you want to date Paul Danberg, isn't it?" Nicky asked, her ice finished.

Sara blushed.

"Now Nicky will tell you to ask him out yourself," I predicted.

Nicky nodded. "Exactly."

"Once and for all, Nicky, I *can't*. It would be humiliating. He probably likes someone else."

Biting another cube of ice, Nicky shook her head and mumbled something that sounded like "nonsense."

I could sympathize with Sara. Her worries were exactly the ones I had about Greg, even after our conversation in the hall. To bring up the subject, I said, "It must be nice to have a date whenever you want it. All Marion has to do is call Burke, and all you, Nicky, have to do is snap your fingers, and every guy in the school comes running."

Marion stared into her soda, making me wonder if I'd managed to say the wrong thing.

I had.

"Going together isn't as simple as all that," she said somberly.

We were all quiet.

"What do you mean?" Nicky whispered, noting the slight tremble in Marion's lower lip.

Marion sighed. "I'm just—I'm afraid it will happen again."

"That *what* will happen again?" Nicky asked, frowning.

"Richard," I explained in a word.

"Oh." Nicky looked worried.

"But, Marion," Sara offered, "Burke is a nice person."

"That's right," Nicky agreed. "He's nothing like Richard Pinson. When you think about it, Richard was a real hotshot. He never went with anybody for more than a month."

"And just think, you and Burke have been together for *three* months," I said brightly.

"That's what worries me," Marion countered.

Nicky leaned forward. "You mean—you think he's getting restless or something."

Marion nodded. "Lots of times he just stares off into space."

"Oh, Mare—" I began, using our old nickname for her.

"And sometimes," she interrupted, "at the movies, or when we go out to eat, he acts as though he's a million miles away."

"Everyone's a million miles away at the movies," I said.

"When you go out to eat, too?" Nicky asked, eyes widening.

"Yes," Marion replied. "Even—even when we kiss." She stared into her soda again.

"Wow!" Nicky gasped.

I shot her a look. She was actually beginning to sound convinced. "What do you mean, 'wow'?" I demanded.

"Well, this was the way it started out with Richard, wasn't it? I mean, there *are* similarities."

"Nicky!" I exploded.

Sara, at least, was on my side. "We shouldn't be comparing Burke to Richard. I think you're still just a little frightened about guys after Richard. After all, it was only last fall that you broke up with him. Maybe you need to give Burke the benefit of the doubt."

"Sara's right," Nicky agreed. "But all I'm saying is that it never hurts to be careful, you know? I mean, guys can be funny. Take Dennis. He's nice and everything. But sometimes—sometimes I just have no idea what he's thinking. I mean, no one ever knows *what* a guy is thinking."

"They're thinking about you," I said. "All guys think about you."

"But what do they think about me, personally? What do they think of any girl personally? Do they ask a girl out because she's cute, or fun to be with, or because she's nice, or what?"

"Nicky," I began, "do you really worry about all this?"

"Well," Nicky said, studying the freckles on her arm, "I don't lose sleep over it, I guess. But I wonder. Sometimes it seems—well, you

14

know—as though guys ask me out just because I'm popular or something." She stared at a freckle and wouldn't look up at us.

"Are you serious, Nicky?" I asked. "I can't *believe* this. Guys ask you out because you're terrific, that's why."

"I second that," Marion said firmly. "I have a reason to feel insecure today. But you don't."

Nicky frowned again. "Sometimes I feel as though people think of me as an airhead."

"An airhead!" I scoffed. "Nicky, that's crazy."

"How do you know? I mean, *you* know the real me. But guys—sometimes they look really put off when I say something even halfway brainy ."

"Men are mysteries." Marion sighed so dramatically that she really could have been acting in a movie.

I sighed, too, and sank back into the booth. There was no sense in telling the gang about Greg now. Given the mood they were in, my excitement over a possible new romance would go over like a lead balloon.

I thought a lot about our conversation on my walk home. Crossing Sierra Street, I decided that Marion was right about one thing. Men *were* mysteries. Nicky was right, too, when she said that you never really knew what a guy was thinking. How, for instance, did I know that Greg's talking to me in the hallway meant anything at all? Maybe he was just being friendly. Maybe he was dating half a dozen other girls and just wanted to add me to the list.

What did I really know about Greg Segura, anyway? He was on the gymnastics team, was one of the smartest kids in our history class, had a nice way of walking and a terrific smile. Those facts gave me plenty to dream about, but not much to act on.

Standing in our kitchen that afternoon, my brother Jake flicked back a shock of his shiny brown hair. "Listen, Allie. I'm the cook today, remember? That means I'm not the maintenance man. *You* oil the front gate."

"But *I'm* the dishwasher today," I shot back. "Which means I'm not the maintenance woman."

Dinnertime at our house causes occasional arguments. A few years before, though, we used to argue every day. That was back when my dad, who's a professional cooking teacher, made all the meals. Mom was in charge of the laundry and odd jobs, and we kids were supposed to do the dishes together. What a joke. The kitchen became a battleground. We threw

16

dishrag torpedos, soapsud salvos—we even sprayed water at each other. Each of us accused the other of not working hard enough. If Jake claimed he had a paper due or an exam to study for, I'd complain that my parents were letting him off easy because he was a boy. If I said I wasn't feeling good or something, Jake would rave that I was getting off easy because I was the baby of the family. It was like World War Three every night.

But that was before we got the System. It was Mom's idea. She gave us a rotating schedule of chores. Dad took to it right away, since he had recently gotten the bright idea that his children would never learn the joy of cooking unless he removed himself from the kitchen.

"Maybe Mom or Dad will oil the stupid gate," Jake muttered. He leaned his long body over the stove to taste the soup he'd been stirring and came up with a smack of satisfaction.

For the zillionth time I wondered how he—a mere two years older than I was—had gotten to be so tall. How come I was still a five-foot-two shrimp? And how come he had gotten Mom's big blue eyes, while I got Dad's boring hazel ones?

"Or maybe," Jake was saying, "they'll just wait till the new one's put in."

"The new what?" I asked, blinking.

He took another slurp of the soup. "The new fence and gate."

I narrowed my eyes. "*What* new fence and gate?"

"Geez, Allie, the one Mom and Dad are thinking about putting in."

I hated it when he acted so superior, as if being a senior in high school meant he shouldn't have to answer questions from a lowly fifteen-year-old like me.

"I didn't hear about any new fence and gate," I persisted. "How come they always tell *you* this stuff, and not me?"

Jake rolled his eyes. "Here we go again. How should I know? I guess you didn't ask."

You didn't ask. That was my family's favorite line. *You didn't ask* whether or not we were going to chop down the old pine tree. *You didn't ask* if we were going to paint the bathroom tangerine. *You didn't ask* was their standard excuse every time they wanted to avoid telling me something. Or even when they just plain *forgot* to tell me. Sure, it was mostly details I missed out on, but I still didn't like being the last in our family to know things.

"Aw, don't look so pitiful," Jake said, giving me a disgusted look. "You usually find out about stuff days before anyone else does, anyway, you little snoop. You're such a busybody—"

"I am not."

"You are so."

"I am not!"

"OK, Double-O Seven," he said, attacking a green pepper with the chopping knife. "Then who was the one who organized the little spy ring to keep tabs on me and my friends? Huh? You and those dopey friends of yours trailed us like bloodhounds."

He was right. I had to smile, remembering the spy club I had started with Marion and Sara back in the fifth grade, the year my family moved to Sequoia Hills. But still, I couldn't let Jake get the upper hand in our argument.

"Jake, if I didn't ask a few questions around here, do you know what would happen? You and Mom and Dad would decide to—to rent out my room, and I wouldn't find out until moving day."

Satisfied that my point was made, I lifted my chin, grabbed an apple from the fruit bowl, and marched upstairs.

To be honest, I knew my parents wouldn't do anything that drastic without consulting me. And I didn't care what color the bathroom was painted or if a new fence was put in. It was back when I was a kid that I had hated not knowing everything. That was one reason I had started the spy ring. Marion and Sara went for the idea right away. For one thing, neither of them had any older brothers. They were spellbound with curiosity about mine. Also, we all desperately wanted to be in on whatever was going on. We began snooping almost as soon as we got to know one another. Never again would I miss out on news.

I sighed as I went into my room, nudging a pile of Agatha Christie paperbacks aside with my foot and thinking about how much my friends and I had changed since the old days. Spying on Jake now would be unbearably dull. There just wasn't much about his life that seemed very interesting. All he ever did was go to school, play tennis, and date a girl on his tennis team. My friends and I had plenty of other things to think about—homework, after-school jobs, future careers, and last but not least, boys.

After plopping down on my bed, I took a bite out of my apple. Boy, did we *ever* think about boys. That was what we talked about the most, anyway. It seemed that they caused more problems for us than anything else. If only we knew what they were thinking, as Nicky had said. Then she wouldn't have to wonder why she was so popular, Marion wouldn't have to doubt Burke, and Sara could figure out how to zoom in on Paul. And I, of course, would know whether or not Greg was really interested in me.

So many questions could be answered. If only—

All of a sudden I stopped chewing on my apple and sat straight up. I was thunder-struck at the idea that had just come into my head.

"No," I whispered. "You couldn't. It's too crazy. Don't even think about it."

But I couldn't help it. My idea was so totally wild and brilliant that I *had* to think about it.

I jumped up and shut the door to my room, locked it, and then took down the little key taped to the back wall of my closet. Reverently I unlocked the bottom drawer of my desk and took out an old, yellowed scrapbook.

A proud feeling tingled over me as I read the carefully drawn blue letters on the cover.

"Mission: Knowledge."

That mission was over. We'd stopped spying on my brother years ago. But this time, *this time* I had a new mission in mind. And I knew just what we could call it.

I took a brand-new folder from my supply drawer and printed a title across the front.

"Mission: Love."

Chapter Two

Of course, I knew I might have a little trouble selling my idea to the gang. Spying on people wasn't easy. It might even be a little risky. But what were our alternatives? How else could Marion find out for sure if Burke was really cheating on her? I, for one, had plenty of faith in Burke. From my point of view, Marion should have been satisfied with his word. But she wasn't. Richard Pinson had hurt her too badly. The only way to prove Burke's loyalty to her was with a little snooping around. Just a little.

It wouldn't be an ongoing thing. Within a month or so, I figured we would know all we wanted to about the habits and attitudes of the guys in question. Namely, Burke, Paul, Dennis, Bob—and Greg. I must admit, the thought of snooping on Greg did make me feel a little queasy, but not enough to call off my idea.

Late afternoon the following Saturday I slipped the old "Mission: Knowledge" scrapbook into a plain brown paper bag and then zipped it up casually into my backpack. No one could possibly suspect what valuable information I was carrying across the neighborhood to Marion's house, where we had all been invited for dinner.

When I got there, I heard Nicky's bubbly laughter coming from Marion's room.

"I guess the party's started," I said to Mrs. Duvall.

"Sounds like it," she agreed. "Go on up, Allie. But remind them, will you, that dinner will be ready soon. I understand you all have plans for tonight, and Marion has a date with Burke, so don't get too carried away."

"Oh, OK. Thanks."

I went quietly up the stairs, thinking about how I was going to tell them about Mission: Love. It would have to be done gently, I knew. I'd have to start by reminding them of all the fun we used to have in our old spy ring.

When I got to Marion's room, I clung to the wall of the hallway and peered in around the door frame.

"Psst!" I hissed.

Marion turned to see who it was.

"Allie, what *are* you doing?"

I dashed into the room and shut the door behind me, which set off Sara's giggles.

"Have you been spying on us?" Nicky asked.

I put my backpack carefully on the bed and dropped down beside it. "Nope. Just practicing for when I do. Your mom says dinner's almost ready, Marion."

"I know," she said. "Burke will be here at seven. Are you and Sara still going to the movies tonight?"

I looked at Sara and nodded. "Far as I know. What are we going to see, anyway?"

"Nicky's got the paper," Sara said. She looked across the room. "Did you find anything interesting?"

Nicky shook her head. "Ben and I are going to that old Hitchcock movie. But you already saw it, didn't you, Allie?"

"Yeah, and I wouldn't want to go along and watch Ben adore you all night, anyway. What else is playing?"

"Here." She handed me the entertainment section. "Take a look."

Standing by the stereo, Marion said, "We were trying to decide what to listen to when you came in. But Sara's reading through college catalogs, so we can't play anything too wild."

"College catalogs?" For a minute, I forgot about the mission. "Wow. Where'd you get them?"

"My sister Sue gave them to me. She sent off for them the year before last, when she was a senior. They might be a little dated."

"Come on," Nicky shouted impatiently. "What's the music going to be?"

"Phil Collins," I suggested and picked up one of the catalogs. "Hey, University of Pennsylvania. Are you thinking about way out there, Sara?"

She shrugged and pushed up her glasses. "Maybe. I hear they have a good prelaw program."

"I don't see how you can be thinking about going anywhere yet," Marion commented as she put on the album. "We're just sophomores, for pete's sake."

"There's nothing wrong with just looking at schools," I said in Sara's defense.

"Yeah," Nicky added. "And we should be prepared when we go into Mrs. Atherton's office for the third degree next fall. She'll probably flip when I tell her I want to go to art school. She's really tough on some kids."

"She's only if you don't know what you want

to do," Sara explained. "If you've got a career choice already, she's not too bad."

I leaned back on Marion's throw pillows. "How about basket weaving? How about if I walk in and say 'Mrs. Atherton, I would like to become a basket weaver. Where should I go for my training?' "

"She'd probably take you seriously," Marion answered. "She has absolutely no sense of humor."

"What *are* you thinking of going into, anyway, Allie?" Sara asked.

"Haven't decided," I said, shrugging.

"I know," Nicky said deadpan. "The CIA."

"I wouldn't be surprised," Marion said with a laugh. "There Sara would be, a famous attorney, getting her clients out of jail. And in would come Allie to arrest her for exposing government secrets or something."

"Ha, ha, ha," I retorted. "That's not even the CIA's job. It would be the FBI. And I wouldn't want to work for either one of them. I'd be a *private* eye."

Just about then I realized it was a perfect time to tell them about my plan, but then Nicky spoke up.

"Hey, that would be great, Allie. We could hire you to do detective work for us. Like if I had priceless jewelry and someone stole it—"

"Or if I wanted information about my client's enemies," Sara said.

"*Or* on your husband," I added dramatically.

All three of them turned to look at me. Their expressions were so curious that I could have sprung my news right then. But I decided to lead them around to it more slowly.

"Look at what I brought over," I said casually. I reached into my backpack and took out the old cardboard folder.

"Oh, wow," Sara whispered. "I haven't seen that in ages!"

"Neither have I," Marion said, smiling. "Where've you been hiding it?"

"Under lock and key."

"Oh," Nicky cried. "Is this the famous spy book I used to hear about?"

"Shh!" I put a finger to my lips. "Do you want the whole neighborhood to find out?"

"Look." Sara was giggling. She pointed to one of the pasted-in scraps of paper. "See how crinkled up this one is? It's because"— she started giggling again—"it's a note from Marion about where we were going to meet to go spying that afternoon. 'The corner, four o'clock. After I read it, I threw it in the trash in social studies. But after class Allie jumped up and ran to the trash can to dig it out."

"Oh, I remember that," Marion said,

smiling. " 'Secrecy is the key,' Allie always said." She held up three fingers, like a Boy Scout and crossed her heart.

"That's not how we did it," Sara corrected. "It was like this. You hold your fingers spread apart, not all together."

Marion repositioned her fingers as Sara had demonstrated. After a moment she went back to leafing through the scrapbook.

"You even had a special salute?" Nicky asked, marveling. "Wow! The most exciting thing *we* ever did in Phoenix was play kick the can."

"Oh, we had a great time," Marion said. "Remember when your mom almost caught us, Allie? It was when we were listening to your brother through the wall with that glass."

"I remember." I nodded. "We tried to look so innocent."

"Look. Here's a note about it." Sara held it up for us. " 'Close call. Glass trick risky.' "

"And about the time we listened to Jake talking on the phone to that girl he liked?"

I waited patiently. At any minute they were going to get the message. One of them would come up with the same idea I'd had. I wouldn't even have to be the one to propose it. They'd figure it out for themselves.

But after ten minutes I saw no flashes pass across anyone's face. They were still reading through the little notes, explaining them all to Nicky.

"You know," she said, "I got here too late. You three had so much fun together! If only I'd moved to Sequoia Hills in the fifth grade instead of eighth. I would have made you guys expand the operation. We could have even spied on my sister. She always picked on me, and I would have loved to find a way to black-mail her with something really juicy."

"We tried spying on my sister once," Sara said. "But it was pretty boring. All she did was talk to her friends on the phone, and we didn't have an extension to listen in on."

I sat cross-legged, tapping my fingers on my knee. My patience was wearing thin. Wasn't it obvious to them yet? Mission: Love was such a great idea, and I'd planted so many clues about it. I couldn't understand why it didn't just jump out at my friends the way it had at me.

I cleared my throat. "We put together some pretty good information then, didn't we?"

Sara nodded. "Here's a great one. 'Jake discusses possible purchase of ten speed'."

"Wouldn't you all agree that discreet spying can be quite useful?" I asked pressing on.

Nicky kept leafing through the book, but Sara and Marion both looked up at me. The time, I figured, was finally right.

"It's so useful," I said. "Don't you think we should start doing it again?"

Then Nicky looked up, too. "Do what?" she asked.

I smiled. "Let's just call it 'information gathering'."

Marion looked at me doubtfully, and Sara peered at me over the tops of her glasses.

"Allie," Marion said slowly, "are you thinking what I think you're thinking?"

I shrugged. "Depends. What are you thinking?"

"That you're crazy."

"Why?" Nicky asked in confusion. "Why is she crazy?"

"She wants us to start spying again," Sara murmured.

Nicky's eyes lit up. "Hey, that's terrific!"

Marion glanced at her. "I don't see what's so terrific about it. We're not children anymore." She lifted her chin.

Cool as a cucumber, I answered, "You're the one with the suspicious mind, Marion."

"What's that supposed to mean?" she shot back.

Sara chewed on her lip.

I sighed and leaned toward Marion. "Listen, Mare. Your problem with Burke is what got this whole idea cooking for me. The rest of us have something to gain from it, too. But you—"

Nicky's gasp cut me off. "You mean—we're going to spy on *Burke*?"

"And Paul Danberg. And Dennis and Bob. And"—I didn't want to mention Greg just then—"whoever else we come up with."

"Allison Perrin-James," Marion began, her tone low and very serious. In her big wicker chair, she looked more regal than ever. "You and I have been friends for five years. I'll admit I've gone along with more than a few of your crazy schemes. But if you think I'll—"

"I think you haven't thought about it enough," I interrupted. "Listen, it'll be easy. We'll be super subtle. All we have to do is place ourselves in strategic positions—and stay alert."

She was shaking her head.

"Marion." I narrowed my eyes at her. "Do you or do you not suspect that Burke is going out with other girls?"

"I don't know," she said flatly and looked away.

"Well, I don't believe he is. But if you're worried about it enough to break down and cry in the Pit, then I think we ought to get busy and do something about it. Otherwise, you'll keep torturing yourself. Plus you'll end up hurting Burke."

When she started biting her lip, I knew I'd struck the right chord. For a few seconds we were all quiet. Then Nicky spoke up, "I'm not really worried about whether or not Dennis or Bob goes out with other girls. Why should we spy on them?"

I sighed in exasperation. "Didn't you say you wanted to know what they were thinking, Nicky? Why they ask girls out?"

"Yeah, but—"

"Well, OK. We'll just listen in a little—in the halls and stuff. Lots of important conversations go on in the halls, you know. Guys talk to each other about girls just as much as we talk about them."

"If not more," Sara added pensively. Then, all of a sudden, she said one word, "Paul."

"Yes," I said eagerly. "We could spy on Paul, too."

She didn't say any more, but I could tell from the look in her eyes what she was thinking.

"Paul won't be hard to figure out," I told her carefully. "All we have to do is watch him, just to see who he looks at—who he talks to."

"This isn't honest!" Marion burst out.

I started to bite on a thumbnail, wondering how to answer her. I had been thinking hard about the problem of honesty ever since I came up with Mission: Love. It wasn't exactly saintly to run around eavesdropping on people. But it wasn't exactly wrong, either. Was it? I had turned the question over and over in my mind but kept coming up with the same answer: our cause was a worthy one. The end results would justify the small amount of sneaking around we'd have to do. Of that I felt sure.

"It's not dishonest, Marion," I finally announced.

"Maybe you don't think so," she snapped. "But I would feel *very* dishonest spying on Burke."

"Then don't," I said and shrugged. "We'll do it for you."

"You'll what?"

"See, it would work better that way. It would arouse fewer suspicions. Burke will be much less likely to notice one of us hanging around than he would you."

She crossed her arms. "I don't like it, Allie."

"Listen," I said firmly. "We are simply going to satisfy our curiosity. There's no real harm in that."

"Curiosity," Márion answered solemnly, "killed the cat."

That shut me up for a little while. I was also bothered by the fact that I was being so hypocritical. Sure, I was perfectly willing to use deceit to find out about my friend's male interests. But what about my own? My conscience kept needling me about how Greg would hate it if we spied on him.

Sara broke the silence. "I'm with you, Allie."

We all stared at her.

"You are?" I whispered. I hadn't expected shy, blushing Sara to volunteer first. "I mean, you are?" I repeated, slowly recovering from the shock. "That's terrific!"

Nicky raised her hand and spread the three fingers apart. "Me, too," she said, giggling. "It sounds like fun. And I'd hate to miss out on all of it again."

"Great! We're in business, then." I turned to look at a severe-looking Marion.

"You're really going through with this, aren't you?" she muttered.

I nodded. "Don't be mad, Mare. I—I understand how you feel, OK? And I think—listen, don't we all agree that Marion doesn't have to join us if she doesn't want to? I mean, we can do the work for her."

"For free, even," Nicky confirmed.

Marion gave us a thoughtful look, then shrugged as if she'd given up on us. "I don't believe you three. You actually intend to go out there and make fools of yourselves. What are you going to do when you get caught?"

"No way will we get caught," I assured her. "All we're going to do is be in the right place at the right time. Just a little harmless eavesdropping, that's all. We won't do anything dramatic."

"You mean you won't try to plant any tape recorders under furniture, as you did that time in your brother's room?" She eyed me suspiciously.

"No, Marion. Of course not."

"Or tap anyone's phone?"

"We don't even know *how*," I countered.

"And you won't question Burke's family and friends?"

"No!"

"Or neighbors?"

I rolled my eyes. "Mare, don't be ridiculous. *Trust* us."

"Yeah, Marion," Nicky added. "We're your best friends, remember?" She sighed and leaned back in her chair.

"Well?" Sara asked expectantly.

Marion glanced at each one of us before

shutting her eyes. When she finally spoke, it was as if she were sentencing us to some awful punishment.

"All right," she whispered. "Do it."

I reached over and gave her hand a quick pat. "You won't be sorry, Marion. Honest."

She sighed again and wouldn't open her eyes.

"OK," I began, trying to ignore Marion's melodramatics. "The first thing we need to do is figure out a plan of action. We have to be organized about this."

"Yes," Sara agreed. "We'll need to take every necessary precaution."

"Hey, I know one thing we can do," Nicky said. "How about if we all set it up so that none of us has to spy on her own guy?"

"Or guys, in some cases," Sara added pointedly.

I nodded. "Great idea, Nicky. That way, we'll really cut down on the chance of discovery. If I'm spying on Burke, for instance, and you're spying on Paul, and Sara's watching Dennis or Bob or whomever for you, they'll *never* get suspicious."

"We could even team up," Sara suggested. "More than one of us could be assigned to the same subject. That way we'd get more information."

I turned to Marion. "See? We're brilliant."

She opened her eyes just wide enough to make them cool ebony slits. "Who," she asked, "is *your* subject, Allison?"

"M-my subject?" I stammered. Sooner or later I was going to have to decide about bringing Greg into our project, but I wanted to make it later. "Um, well, Burke, of course. I'll take him over for you."

She shook her head. "I mean, who will Sara and Nicky snoop on for *you*?"

"Oh." I swallowed hard. "For me?" All three of them were watching me closely.

Then Nicky grinned. "How about John Mathers? He still likes you."

"Are you kidding?" I grimaced. "He could spend the rest of his life glued to a Pac-Man machine for all I care!"

"I know who it is," Sara said quietly.

My heart thumped. Did she really know? If she did, how had she found out?

"It's Bruce Irwin. He danced with you a lot at the Valentine's Day party, and I bet you want to know if he still likes Melissa Beebe."

I relaxed. "No, Sara. It's not Bruce Irwin."

"There must be someone, Allie. Come on, tell us." Nicky was almost as bad about secrets as I was.

"Well," I hedged, squirming. "Maybe there will be. Just not right now."

I couldn't bring myself to add Greg's name to our sneaky little list. Not for a while, anyway.

"I mean," I explained, "I'll help you guys first, then we can worry about me. We'll have our hands full with Burke and Paul and all of your guys."

They didn't seem to believe me, so I tried to distract them. Maybe they'd give up easily. "Now, how about our strategy? How are we going to set this up?"

They did give up easily. Maybe they were too involved in thinking about their own problems to grill me further.

Sara answered first. "I think we should keep a careful log of our findings, like the old one."

Smugly, I pulled out the new notebook.

" 'Mission: Love!' " Nicky cried when she saw the cover. "How perfect. I love it!"

"But if we're going to keep a document like this," I warned, holding it up to make my point, "we'll have to be very careful. I mean, we can't leave it around in a place where someone might find it."

"Then don't keep it," Marion suggested crossly.

Nicky pouted. "But that's no fun."

"Fun," said Marion, "is not the object of this mission. And you're all intelligent enough to remember what you've seen, aren't you? So why write it down? Why keep a piece of incriminating evidence like that just so you can giggle over it?"

I sighed. "OK, Mother Marion. You win. No log book for Mission—"

"Girls!" The door to Marion's room opened.

For a second I was frozen. Then I clutched the notebook to my chest to hide the cover.

"Dinner time," Mrs. Duvall said with a smile as she peeked in at us.

As soon as she left, we all sighed. It was as if we'd been caught plotting a murder, not a simple spying.

"See?" Marion whispered. "You've already made nervous wrecks out of us, Allie. What will we be like after we've been doing this for a while?"

"Well informed," I shot back and jumped off the bed. "Now, where can I put this till after dinner?"

"Do you swear you'll get rid of it then?" Marion asked, squinting at me.

I rolled my eyes, then raised my hand in our three-fingered salute. "On my honor."

We hid the 'Mission: Love' notebook under a pile of sweaters in her dresser. At least for a while no one would be able to guess what we'd been up to.

Chapter Three

We were sitting in our favorite ice-cream place, Ice Delight. Sara sank a spoon into her very berry sundae and put it listlessly into her mouth.

"Such an exciting way to spend Saturday night," I said, stirring my double fudge and chip shake.

"Fascinating," she agreed.

Someone dropped a quarter into the jukebox and put on a Duran Duran song that rumbled and shook all the booths, even ours in the back corner.

"We didn't even get a good table," I complained.

"Who cares? We don't know anyone here tonight, anyway."

I glanced over my shoulder at the crowded

shop. "Looks like family night. They must have advertised with those two-for-one coupons in the paper."

"Probably," Sara agreed. "We're the only people here between the ages of seven and thirty-five."

We ate our ice cream in silence for a couple of minutes. I noticed that the girl who made my shake had thrown in some extra chocolate chips. It perked me up some, but not much.

"Wasn't it about an hour and a half ago that we stuffed ourselves at Marion's?" I wondered aloud.

Sara glanced at her watch. "One hour and twenty-two minutes."

"So why are we doing it again?"

"What else is there to do?" she asked, resting her chin in her palm. "Marion is out with Burke, Nicky's out with Ben, and here we are."

"We could go to my house and play Scrabble," I suggested halfheartedly.

"Like last week, and the week before."

"Scrabble does have one advantage, Sara."

"What?"

"It doesn't have any calories."

That, at least, made her grin.

It really wasn't bad spending Saturday nights with Sara. If I couldn't be out with some gorgeous guy, I was glad I was with her.

She had been my first friend in Sequoia Hills, even before Marion. And she was still one of my three absolute *best* friends.

The trouble was, Sara and I had already spent years together. We knew each other inside out. Going somewhere with a person like that is a little like going out with your favorite pair of pajamas.

"You know," she said seriously, "we really shouldn't be feeling so sorry for ourselves."

"Yes, Sara. I know. I can hear my mother's favorite speech: 'We have roofs over our heads, food on the table, and plenty of constructive, educational activities at our disposal.' I guess we should be volunteering at the hospital, or something."

"We probably should, but that's not what I meant." She leaned forward. "I was talking about the plan. You know. *Your* plan."

"Oh," I said, starting to smile. "The mission."

Sara nodded. "First, I think Marion's right. It *is* dishonest. Or at least pretty underhanded."

I rolled my eyes. "Not this again."

"But," she added quickly, "I think it's worth it. I mean, it's not as if we're planning to publish our information in the *Sequoia Hills Register* or anything. And I don't know what else I could do—about—Paul." His name came out in a whisper. After taking a quick glance around at the tables near our booth, she whispered, "I really like him, Allie. Did you know that he placed first in that debate tournament before Christmas?"

"Of course I know. Everyone in the school knows." Once again, I felt guilty. There Sara was, baring her soul about whom *she* liked, and I couldn't bring myself to breathe a word about Greg.

"The important thing," she went on, "is that we are actually going to start doing something constructive about our—"

"Boring Saturday nights," I finished for her.

"Well, yes. It's not that—you know—I like being with you, Allie, but—"

"I'm not Paul."

She nodded, staring into her sundae. "I feel bad about feeling this way."

"Huh? What are you talking about?"

"Well, my sister complains that girls don't value each others' friendships enough. She says lots of girls don't think twice about breaking a date with a girlfriend if a guy asks them out.

I shrugged. "I guess that would be pretty rude."

"And she says I worry too much about getting dates."

"Don't we all?"

"Not Nicky." Sara's eyes, almost the same light shade of brown as her hair, looked sadder than I'd ever seen them.

"Well, that's the truth," I said sympathetically. "Nicky has *never* worried about getting dates."

"Sue says I don't have enough self-confidence. She says that if I like myself, other people will like me, too."

"I like you, Sara."

She looked up and smiled, and I understood what Sue was trying to say a little better. Having good friends—friends like Sara and Nicky and Marion—was just as important as meeting boys.

Suddenly the sound of boys' laughter burst across the restaurant. Sara's gaze flew toward the door, and I turned to see who was making all the noise.

What I saw made my jaw drop open. I watched for a few thrilled seconds, then snapped my eyes back to my shake.

"Isn't it amazing that three guys can make so much noise?" Sara commented. "I'm surprised that someone hasn't gotten angry—Allie, what's wrong?"

I looked up and tried to seem calm. "Nothing."

"But you're all red, and you—" Suddenly her face relaxed. She nodded wisely. "Oh, I see."

I took a casual sip from my shake. "You see what?"

"I see who's been on your mind."

My blush must have gone about ten times redder.

"So, it's one of those three, isn't it?" Sara said smugly. "It's either Lawrence Kramer, Greg Segura, or Jim Ryba." She thought for a moment. "I give up, Allie. Which one?"

All I could think about was the fact that Greg was just a few yards away from me, ordering a cone. Greg—with his cute freckled nose and that gymnast's glide in his walk. He was wearing his cable knit sweater with the chain of reindeer across the back, too.

What would stop him, I wondered, from walking casually over to our booth, smiling handsomely, and slipping in beside me?

"It's Jim," Sara whispered, snapping me out of my daydream.

I looked at her blankly.

"Ah-hah!" she cried. "I knew it."

"Sara, calm down."

"But why didn't you tell me, Allie? I'll be happy to watch Jim Ryba for you."

"Sara, you—" Before I could go on, I clamped my mouth shut. What was wrong with letting Sara think she was right? For a while, anyway.

I was saved from having to make a decision because in the next instant Sara was whispering again.

"They're leaving." Her pale skin flushed with color. "Jim has a double scoop of mocha mix. Lawrence has a single of chocolate, and Greg has an almond vanilla double cone."

I leaned back and shook my head. "You heard their orders at this distance?"

Sara nodded. "Amazing hearing often compensates for poor vision."

"OK, then," I said as a joke, "now tell where they're headed."

Very quickly, I realized I'd said the wrong thing. Sara—our shy, timid Sara—had taken me seriously. She was ablaze with the fire of Mission: Love.

"Let's find out," she whispered, straightening her glasses. "Come on."

"Come on where?"

She let out an exasperated sigh. "To follow them, of course. This is our chance, Allie."

"But we can't," I said, stalling. "We don't have a plan yet. And I haven't finished my—"

"Hurry!" She grabbed my arm and pulled.

Sara was much stronger than I would have expected of her five-foot-nothing, ninety-four-pound frame. "They're leaving!"

In seconds we were on our way out the door.

This, I thought, *is going to be a new kind of Saturday night.*

Teenage boys, when on foot and in a group, do not move quickly. That was one of the first observations that Sara and I made as we followed our targets to the Remington Theater. They stopped at practically every shop window to point and laugh. Jim found it necessary to swing around all the lamp posts. Lawrence had this thing about checking the time left on parking meters. Greg, I thought proudly, was the only one who seemed at all concerned about getting anywhere. But even his pace was slow and lazy.

"Wait!" Sara whispered, suddenly grabbing my arm and pulling me into the shadows of a storefront. "Don't move or they'll see us."

The boys had all stopped. They stood in front of the theater just twenty yards ahead of us.

"What are they doing?" she whispered, peering through her thick glasses into the dim light.

"Taking out their wallets," I whispered

back. "It looks as if they're checking to see how much money they have."

"Oh. They're going to the movies?" Sara asked glumly.

"Looks like it. Well, I guess that's it for spying tonight, huh? Let's go home."

"But, Allie," she said steadily, "there's nothing to do at home. Remember?"

After the boys went into the theater, she dragged me down the street to get in line. About halfway there I glanced up at the marquee, and froze in my tracks.

"Sara, would you look at what's playing?"

Godzilla Meets the Smog Monster glared down at us in big black letters. There were also big green posters of Godzilla all over the front of the theater.

"Oh" was all Sara said.

She squinted at one of the posters. The star of the show was rearing up in fury.

"Looks great, doesn't it?" I muttered.

"Maybe it's not too bad. For a monster movie, I mean."

"*All* monster movies are bad," I replied and turned to go.

Sara's iron grip caught me again. "One monster movie will not kill you, Allison."

"It will, too. I hate monster movies."

"But you like Jim." Her eyes softened, making her look more like the Sara most people knew. "I understand, Allie. You're nervous, right?"

I looked away. What kind of person was I, anyway? How could I lie that way to one of my best friends? I did not like Jim Ryba, at least not in the way she thought I did. And allowing her to think I did made me feel terribly guilty. But not guilty enough to confess. As bad as I felt, spying on Jim Ryba also allowed me to spy on Greg Segura, which was not a bad way to spend Saturday night.

"Don't worry," Sara was saying. "He won't see us. We'll be careful, OK?"

Before I could talk her out of it, she had bought us both tickets.

As we entered the darkened theater, she whispered. "Do you see them?"

I pointed to the front row.

"Perfect!" she cried.

It did not seem at all perfect to me. How could I ever date a boy who sat in the front row in theaters? Or, for that matter, one who paid good money to see Godzilla movies? The course of our romance unfolded in my mind. First I would go nearsighted. Then I would start having nightmares about giant lizards and air pollution.

"Allie, come on," Sara urged. "This is great.

Now we can sit wherever we want, and still see them."

"So what?" I whispered back. "They won't be talking about girls during the movie. And even if they did, we couldn't hear unless we sat right behind them."

That did not matter to Sara. If I hadn't known her better, I might have thought she actually enjoyed watching Godzilla trounce the Smog Monster. She barely budged during the whole movie, sitting with her mouth half-open, staring at the screen. But the movie finally ended, and a bunch of foreign-name credits rolled up.

Right about then, I noticed Jim and Lawrence and Greg standing up.

"They're leaving!" Sara whispered urgently.

"I know."

"Look this way," she ordered. "Toward the wall, so he won't see you."

I obeyed, while Sara kept one eye on the guys. As soon as they were well past us, we jumped up and mixed with the crowd behind them. A couple of times Greg turned his head to say something to Jim and Lawrence, giving me a glimpse of his cute profile. It made me want to call out to him, or at least run up for a closer look.

"Hey, Sara! Allie!"

Someone tapped me on the back. I turned around to see two familiar faces.

"Dennis! Bob!" I exclaimed. "What are you doing here?"

"That's what we were about to ask you." Dennis grinned. "Nicky with you?"

I shook my head. "You're out of luck, guys. Sorry to break your hearts."

Sara leaned over and muttered in my ear, "The ever-faithful Nicky Gould fan club."

I nodded and snickered, then turned my eyes forward again to look for Greg. We had reached the lobby, and the crowd fanned out in all directions.

"Sara," I asked, "where is he?"

"Who?"

I don't think Sara was trying to trick me, but she almost did anyway. I almost slipped and said Greg's name. "Lawrence and Greg and Jim," I whispered.

Her eyes searched the crowd in front of us. "Why, I just saw them a second ago."

"Darn! They're gone!"

"Who is?" Dennis asked from just behind me.

"Oh," I said, "the um, the—"

"Junior Mints," Sara replied, jabbing me in the ribs.

I picked up on the fib. "Yeah. We had some, but I guess we ate them all."

"Here, have some of mine," Bob offered, holding out the box. "Help yourself."

"Oh, no thanks, Bob. We're in a big hurry," I answered, then raced with Sara for the front door.

From a shadowy spot next to the box office, we scanned the whole crowd. Our targets were still nowhere in sight.

"We should at least be able to see Greg. If they're here, that is," Sara commented. "That reddish hair usually stands out."

"True," I said. "But I don't see them anywhere on the street, either."

"Darn!"

I did a double take at Sara. "Darn" was about the strongest language I had ever heard her use. In fact, I hardly ever saw her act as daring as she had that evening. If nothing else, at least Mission: Love was livening her up a little.

I smiled and touched her arm. "Hey, don't worry about it. It was fun while it lasted, right? I mean, we have to keep Mission: Love in perspective. We can't start taking it too seriously."

"I agree." Sara nodded. "This could get out of hand."

"Anyway," I went on, trying to lighten things up, "gorgeous, fascinating girls like us don't need to spy on guys to get boyfriends, right?"

Sara turned her brown eyes to me. I saw the corner of her mouth begin to tip upward. Mine followed, and pretty soon we were both laughing.

But our giggles didn't last for long. Once more, Sara's fingers closed tightly around my arm.

"Look," she whispered. "It's them!"

I scanned the sidewalk for Greg's beautiful auburn hair.

Sara pointed across the street. "Bob and Dennis!"

"Oh, them." I nodded in disappointment.

I looked at Sara and knew immediately what she was thinking. Her eyes glowed.

"OK, OK," I said. "Mission: Love Target Group Number Two. Subjects: Dennis Conroy and Bob Lopez. Purpose: to investigate their interest in one Nicky Gould."

She laughed, "Well, don't you think it's a good idea?"

I shrugged. "I guess. We'd better hurry, though. They're going into the video arcade."

By the time we crossed the street, Bob and Dennis had already entered Time Zone. Sara sneaked a peek in through one of the neon-lit windows. "This place is very small, Allie."

"Yeah," I agreed. "But it has enough games in it that we can make ourselves scarce."

"But I don't like video games."

"And *I* don't like monster movies," I countered. "Come on."

Sara was right about Time Zone. It was so small that only the crowd and a row of machines down the middle gave us any hope for not being seen.

"Psst!" I motioned to her after we went in. "Over here."

The pinging noises and flashing lights overwhelmed her. She didn't move.

"Sara!" I whispered again.

She followed me along the edge of the room.

"What are our targets playing?" Sara asked.

"Looks as though Dennis is playing Donkey Kong, and Bob is over by the Millipede game."

"What if they see us?" she asked again.

I rolled my eyes. Where had her nerve and daring disappeared to? "They won't," I assured her. "Look, they're on the middle row of machines. We'll stay over here in the corner, OK?"

After watching them in silence for a while, I grumbled, "They sure do milk those quarters."

"Does that mean they're good?"

I frowned at her. "Of course it does. You've honestly never played a video game before?"

"Honestly."

"Never?"

"Never." She lifted her chin defiantly. "Entirely by choice."

"Oh, Sara, don't be so stuck up. Some of them are fun."

"They rot the brain."

"Come on. One little video game won't kill you. Look, here's Missile Command. This game is hard to find these days."

"Allie!" she hissed. "We're on duty!"

"Those two guys aren't going to budge for a while, Sara. We might as well have a little fun while we wait."

I ended up spending two dollars in quarters. Every time I handed the controls to Sara, she'd act disgusted and ended up letting all her cities get destroyed.

"No more," she finally insisted. "You play. I'll watch the guys."

"OK." I used my last quarter. Certainly I wasn't the best Mission Command player around, but I was pretty good. John Mathers, my old boyfriend, had been a real champ at it. I must have watched him play about fifty times. When people started turning to other games, I stayed with Missile Command, and that's how I got better at it. At least I had gotten something out of dating John.

I was already up to eighty thousand points when I first heard Sara whisper my name. I ignored her for a minute because I was busy picking off smart bombs. Just a couple more, and I'd win another bonus city. I concentrated hard and managed to hit them all perfectly. It was terrific! The screen lit up with my bonus points, and the machine played a little song for me. I was really on a roll.

"Allie!" Sara hissed again in a much more urgent voice.

"Just a minute," I muttered back.

The missiles were coming at me again. Just then I couldn't have cared less about Bob and Dennis. Whatever Sara had to report on them paled in comparison to the excitement of Missile Command. I had never played so well in my life.

After a minute I noticed some movement around me and figured that Sara had inched closer to Dennis and Bob for a better view. *Good work*, I thought and kept playing.

Then I realized someone was standing beside me again. I figured Sara'd come back, but she's barely a hundred pounds, and the someone standing next to me was larger. And out of the corner of my eye, I spotted a hand on the game machine. It was a large, boyish hand. I recognized that hand from hours of observation in history class.

I looked up at Greg, and my missile base went up in smoke.

Chapter Four

"Oh, you got wiped out!"

Greg's eyes were on the glowing remnants of my city, but my eyes were on him. I stared at the silky brown curl of his eyelashes. I had to keep staring to make sure it was really him.

So *he* was what Sara had tried to warn me about! When his gaze turned away from the screen toward me, I got more of a thrill than I ever had playing Missile Command.

"Yes," I said, sounding shocked. "I guess I did."

"But, wow, Allie, take a look at that score," he said. "You got over a hundred and sixty thousand!"

I followed his gaze back to the screen. There, in big green numbers, was my score: one six three, nine seven five.

"You probably would have scored a lot higher," he added, "if I hadn't startled you. Sorry about that."

"Oh, you didn't—I mean, it's not your fault."

Greg smiled. I still couldn't believe that he was standing right next to me. After all the spying on him that Sara and I had just done, he had actually come over to talk to me.

At that point I noticed Sara standing with Jim and Lawrence, trying to look as if she hung out in video arcades every night.

"Have you been practicing a lot?" Greg asked before I could catch her eye.

I shrugged. "On and off for a couple of years. I think the reason my score is so high is that this game isn't very popular anymore. Not many people take the time to get good at it."

"Modesty, modesty." His grin was not exactly dazzling. His teeth were even a little crooked in front. But what made Greg's smile so wonderful was the way it lit up his whole face. It gave him little crinkles at the edges of his eyes, and it made them sparkle.

I laughed and said, "Really, I don't score this high every time. Tonight's just lucky." *In more ways than one,* I thought.

"In that case," Greg answered, "maybe if I hang around you, I'll get lucky, too. Want to try some Battle Zone?"

"Sure!" I answered, so happy I could hardly speak. But then I remembered Sara. I couldn't abandon her.

"Hey, Sara," I called as casually as possible. "Want to watch Greg and me play?"

Her eyes were as big as saucers. She looked as shocked as she had when we'd first walked into Time Zone. Most likely she was every bit as surprised as I was that our spying assignments had just walked right up and talked to us.

Jim Ryba answered for her. "She's going to stay here with us. Lawrence and I are going to make a Defender champ out of her. Right, Sara?"

I felt awful for her. The look on her face was one of total, helpless confusion. Not only did she hate video games, but I was sure she felt worried by the fact that I was with Greg instead of Jim.

Lawrence gave her a chummy slap on the back, which she answered with a weak smile. I tried to look reassuring, then followed Greg to the Battle Zone machine.

It wasn't long before I'd completely forgotten about poor Sara stuck in her Defender lesson with Jim and Lawrence. Although playing video games is not the most romantic way to spend an evening with the boy of your dreams, just being with Greg was pretty wonderful.

Needless to say, having Greg around made me forget all about our other spying targets. After about a dozen rounds of Battle Zone, though, I looked over Greg's shoulder to see them leaving. That brought me back down to reality. I remembered my faithful spying partner. I saw her still standing in front of the Defender machine, flanked by Jim and Lawrence. She was actually grinning. A shy grin, of course, but there it was. Relief swept over me. Maybe Sara wasn't too miserable, after all. Maybe she was even enjoying the attention from the guys. As a matter of fact, I decided, she should enjoy it. Having some fun with guys would be good for her.

"Don't worry about your friend," Greg said, following my gaze. "Those two guys are experts at Defender. She's in good hands."

I liked the way he'd said it—not in a boasting tone, just matter-of-fact. I realized that he hadn't tried to tell me how to play Missile Command, either. There were some guys who would insist on giving a girl pointers, no matter how well she was doing on her own. I thought that he sure was making up for liking monster movies.

I could have stayed there forever, noticing

more terrific things about Greg, but I realized it was getting late. I craned my neck to look at his watch.

"Eleven-fifteen," he told me, looking at his wrist. "Wow! Where'd that hour go?"

I shrugged, knowing I must be blushing. I was thrilled that Greg could lose track of time while he was with me!

"Would you and Sara like a ride home?" he asked. "I won't have my license for a few weeks, but Jim's got his car."

My heart jumped. He actually wanted to spend *more* time with me!

"Oh, thanks," I answered as calmly as possible. "But we left Sara's car out by Ice Delight."

"Really? That's where we're parked."

"Oh," I didn't say more, for fear of giving away the fact that we'd been following them. I knew exactly where Jim's car was.

"Well, how about if we all walk together?" he offered.

I didn't want to appear too excited, but I must have seemed reluctant because he shrugged and shuffled his feet. "I mean, since we're all going in the same direction—"

"Oh, that sounds great," I said quickly. I gave him a smile that I hoped showed I was anything but reluctant to spend more time with him.

*　　*　　*

Our walk down Shepherd Avenue was not romantic, but it was fun. The glow of happiness stayed with me all night long. When I woke up Sunday morning, I still felt warm and happy.

I've always loved waking up on Sunday mornings because I don't have to get up right away. I can go back to sleep if I want. Or if I'm hungry, there's always one of Dad's weird but interesting Sunday-morning breakfasts waiting in the kitchen. And after that I can just go back to bed. I may have loads of homework due on Monday, but I never look at it until the afternoon. Our family's chore schedule is set up so that no one but Dad has anything to do on Sunday mornings. And the only reason he makes breakfast is because he likes to "create" in peace and quiet.

Jake always sleeps late on Sunday, too, until at least eleven. So his stereo and the TV are silent. And my mom stays in bed to read the detective and mystery novels we both love. The house is deliciously calm.

On that particular morning the silence felt especially wonderful. Through my window the clouds looked gray, but I was sure they were lined with silver. My chipped-up old furniture and the stains on my ceiling, put there by my brother with an exploding bottle of soda, were not the least bit depressing. Everything made me happy. The gray day and my wobbly desk and the brown patches decorating my ceiling were all a part of a wonderful world. And that, of course, included Greg.

I did not go back to sleep. How could I sleep another wink when I could be awake and thinking about Greg Segura? As I jumped out of bed and pulled on my bathrobe, I wondered how I could be so excited about one little hour of playing video games and a short walk with him. I mean, it wasn't as if he had professed eternal love for me. But I could tell—I could just tell that he liked me as much as I liked him. It was in the way he hesitated when he said good night. And in the way he looked embarrassed around his friends, as if he knew they'd tease him about me later. Filled with hope, I flew down the hall on my way to the kitchen.

"Allie?" Mom called to me from her bedroom.

I peeked around the door. "Morning."

"Good morning, honey." Her hair was a mass of uncombed curls, and her glasses, as usual, teetered at the very tip of her nose. Sometimes I wondered how, wearing those huge, clumsy frames, she ever managed to read all the contracts and briefs at her job as a paralegal. "Come talk to me," she said.

She patted a place on the bed next to her, and I sat down.

"Which one is this?" I asked, pulling at the mystery paperback she held.

"The Night of the Seven Suns."

"Oh, boy!" I said. "Let me read it as soon as you're through. Have you figured out what the Seven Suns are yet?"

She shook a finger at me. "No. And you know I wouldn't tell you if I had."

It was our little game. I always tried to trap Mom into giving me clues about the plot, and she always resisted.

"By the way," I asked casually, "how come nobody told me about the new fence?"

Mom looked up from the book with a puzzled frown. "What new fence?"

"Jake said you and Dad are thinking about getting one," I explained.

"Oh, that," She took off her glasses and yawned. "We were just considering it, trying to decide whether or not we have the money. Probably not."

"Oh."

Again, I had to admit that most of the family decisions I complained about getting left out of were less than earthshaking. I wouldn't have been very excited over mulling over the pros and cons of a new fence, anyway. And deep down I knew that if anything important did come up, I would be told. Mom and Dad would never plan anything big without me, I thought.

She must have noticed the serious look on my face. "Things at school going all right, honey?"

"Fine," I answered. Thinking about school made me think about Greg. The look on my face changed to dreamy.

My mother noticed my faraway expression. "Well? Anything special going on?"

I blushed. "Sort of."

"Like what?" she urged.

"Oh, nothing much," I mumbled, picking the lint off her quilt. "Just—I kind of like this guy, and Sara and I ran into him and his friends at the video arcade last night."

Mom smiled. "So when do we get to meet him?"

"Oh, Mother!" I groaned. "I'm not going to marry him. We're just friends."

She laughed and squeezed my hand. "OK. But do I get to find out his name?"

"Greg Segura," I said. "He's in my class and on the gymnastics team, and he's very nice." I gave her a quick peck on the cheek, jumped up, and escaped to the kitchen.

My dad was so involved in creating his latest culinary masterpiece that I didn't get too many questions from him. The kitchen was alive with fruity and spicy smells.

"Morning, Allie-gator," he said, using his favorite nickname for me. "Sleep well?"

"Wonderfully," I stood on my tiptoes to kiss his flour-dusted cheeks.

My father does not fit the image of a professional cook. His students at Quintessential Cuisine always do a double take when they meet him. He stands about six foot three, weighs two hundred pounds, and has the shoulders of a linebacker. In fact, he used to be a linebacker in college.

"Look," he whispered, nodding toward the thick purple sauce bubbling on the stove. His dark eyes lit up. "For blueberry blintzes."

"Mmm." I leaned over to take a whiff of the sauce and to examine the stack of crepe-type shells he had already grilled. "Smells wonderful!"

The blintzes were delicious. I was enjoying my third scrumptious bite when the phone rang. My mother answered it in the bedroom and called down to me. "For you, Allie."

I was still so wrapped up in my general Sunday morning contentment that I didn't bother to wonder who it might be.

"Hello?" I answered on the kitchen phone.

Marion's voice came through loud and clear. "So there's no special boy, huh, Allie?"

Wow, I thought, *news travels fast.* There had been only one flaw with the night before. Sara had figured out why I'd spent the evening talking with Greg instead of with Jim. And it was obvious that she had told Marion right away.

"Allie," my dad cut in. "Don't let those blintzes get cold now, OK?"

I shook my head and shoveled in another mouthful. He smiled.

"Stop chewing into the phone," Marion demanded.

"Sorry."

I suppose you're going to tell me that you and Greg are just friends," she said icily.

"That's right," I mumbled through a mouthful of sour cream and blueberries. "We're just friends."

"Humph. That's not how I heard it. You sneaky thing, Allison Perrin-James. You were willing to spy on every boy but your own."

"But he's not my own, Mare." I tried to keep my voice low in case my father heard me.

"He will be soon," she countered. "From what I hear."

Her certainty gave me a flush of pleasure. Sara, too, had told me on the way home that she thought Greg liked me. I sighed. "Well, I guess I wouldn't complain if you were right. I'm, um, sorry I didn't tell you about him earlier."

She echoed my sigh. "You're forgiven. I'm just mad that you didn't think twice about spying on *our* guys, but you kept yours a secret."

I laughed. "I know. I was feeling pretty guilty about it, too."

"You should have. Now tell me, how long has this relationship been going on?"

"Relationship?" I laughed, then told her about staring at the back of Greg's head in history class.

"Well," said Marion wistfully after hearing my story, "I'm very happy for you, Allie."

"Uh-oh. Is that a note of sadness I detect?"

"No," she answered with another sigh. "Not sadness. At least, not much."

"Oh, Marion. Come on, now. There's no reason for you to feel sad about Burke. We are going to *prove* that to you."

Right away the wheels started turning inside my head. Mission: Love had to get to work—and soon.

Chapter Five

"Look, there's his car!" Nicky exclaimed as she drove us into the Shop 'n' Save parking lot Tuesday afternoon.

I nodded. "Marion said he'd be here."

"But that Marion." Nicky shook her head. "She might have told us Burke worked today just to throw us off track."

"Marion wouldn't do that."

Nicky found a parking space on the far side of the lot. "Why not? She hates this spying stuff."

I smiled. "Don't be fooled. Didn't you notice that gleam in her eye yesterday when I suggested we make Burke our official target this week? She didn't exactly look upset about it, did she?"

"No, I guess she didn't. But she sure acted that way." Nicky pointed out.

"*Acted* is the key word."

I thought back to our talk the day before. Marion tried so hard to appear casual about her problem with Burke, but the truth was that she was terribly scared.

"You want to spy on Burke at his job?" she had asked, eyes wide.

"Well, sure," I answered. "Work would be the perfect place for him to flirt with girls."

Right away I realized how tactless my comment had been. Marion's face was clouded over with sadness.

"I mean, *if* he were going to flirt, of course," I said quickly. "Which we all know he wouldn't."

"Then why go at all?" she shot back.

"To provide you with *proof.*"

And that was exactly what I intended to do. Stupid Richard Pinson had shattered Marion's confidence, and I was determined to build it back up.

Nicky broke into my thoughts. "Too bad Sara couldn't come, too. That would have been even more fun."

"Yeah. Spying with Sara is an experience, all right. But she wouldn't miss a flute lesson for anything. OK, let's review our plan."

"Check," Nicky answered. "Rule number one, always follow a plan. First we'll sneak up to the door and peek in to pinpoint the target's position. Depending on what that is, we'll post ourselves in well-concealed spots for surveillance."

"That's the part I'm still worried about," I said, frowning. "In a grocery store, where can we hide?"

"Oh, we'll find someplace." Nicky opened her door. "Let's go."

She was flushed, and I recognized on her face the same kind of excitement that Sara had worked herself into on Saturday night.

Burke turned out to be right where Marion had said he'd be, manning a register at the front of the store. Marion had told us that Tuesday would be the best day to watch him since he worked the stockroom on other afternoons.

"I guess we'd better go in through the side door, huh?" Nicky asked.

I nodded. "That way he'll have his back to us."

We went around the building to the Borrego Street entrance.

"Oh, Allie." Nicky was giggling when we got there. She put a hand over her heart.

"What's the matter?"

"Well, do you realize," she asked breathlessly, "that this is my first mission?"

I had to grin. "I guess it is."

"I'm so nervous. What if—what if I start to panic or get a giggling fit or something?"

"Shh!" I ordered. "Just don't think about it. You'll do fine."

She took a deep breath to steady herself, then joined me in peering through the glass door at Burke.

"He's busy ringing up that sale," I said. "Let's go in."

"Where will we hide?"

I scanned the rows of groceries. For a first mission, this sure was a toughie. If we hid too far away from Burke, we wouldn't really be able to monitor his reactions to young female customers. But we couldn't get close, either.

"Look!" Nicky cried. "That stack of cereal boxes!"

"What about it?"

"I was in here with my mom on Saturday, and I remember how it's set up. It's sort of like a letter H, with the sides jutting out into the aisle. Just perfect for hiding!"

The display was huge, all right, and smack up in the front.

"See? Isn't it great?" she asked.

"Perfect," I agreed.

"I'll go up the other aisle. That way we'll each be on one side of the H, all right?"

"But how will we communicate? Remember rule number two? Never split up."

Nicky grinned. "You'll see."

I shrugged. "OK, partner."

We giggled and gave each other our special three-fingered salutes. Then I set off down the aisle with the desperate hope that Burke would stay so busy that he wouldn't have a chance to look up and see his girlfriend's best friends scurrying along the rows of cornflakes and canned fruits.

When I reached the Crunch-O display at the end, I found a terrific litte corner to hide in—exactly as Nicky had promised.

"Psst!"

I froze. Were the cereal boxes speaking to me?

"Hey, over here!"

I turned cautiously, recognizing the voice. It sounded strange, as if it were coming through a tunnel. But it was definitely Nicky's.

"I'm in here!" she repeated.

Her voice *was* coming through a tunnel— one that ran right through the middle of the cereal boxes.

"What—" I gasped, seeing her face at the end of it.

Nicky gave me a conspiratorial wink. "The architect got fancy," she whispered.

That was for sure. Right in the center of the stacked boxes, someone had left a hole that you could have put your arm through. All I saw of Nicky was her nose and up, but that was enough for communicating. We got so busy snickering and making faces at each other that for a minute we forgot about the mission. It was Burke's voice on the store loudspeaker that jolted us.

"Price check, please," he called. "Lazzaro Spaghetti Sauce, regular jar."

"Hey," I whispered at Nicky, "we'd better get back to work."

She nodded. "Happy spying!"

For a while my spying was happy. The view of Burke couldn't have been better. I could see him smile at his customers, then turn to his register and ring up the stuff. Although I couldn't hear all the words he said, it was easy to fill in the gaps. "Afternoon, sir. Yes, these bananas are nice. Thank you. Come back and see us again." For a while Burke's customers were a lot older than us—not exactly the people we were interested in seeing him with. And there is only so much checkout counter small talk one can observe with interest. Soon, I started shifting from one foot to the other.

Then I started worrying. What if the manager or someone happened to notice us? Wouldn't they think it strange for two teenage girls to be standing in the corner of a Crunch-O display for ten minutes?

I took a peek through the tunnel looking for Nicky, ready to tell her we should move or something. Not finding her, I glanced back at Burke. Quickly I stopped thinking about moving. What I saw made my eyes nearly pop out of my head.

Lydia Marshall was waiting in Burke's line.

Out of all the girls in Sequoia Hills who could have walked up to Burke's checkout lane, he got Lydia Marshall. What luck! She was Lomitas High's top flirt. If Burke could resist her, then he could resist anyone!

I wanted to signal to Nicky, just to make sure she was watching. But I couldn't take my own eyes off the action.

Lydia was there with Marci McDonald, her sidekick and accomplice in flirting. What any girl could want in the way of looks and clothes, those two had—Lydia, with her dark, smooth skin and huge, brown eyes, Marci, a Christie Brinkley lookalike in every way. While they waited, they thumbed through fashion magazines. Every now and then they'd let out little laughs as high and sweet as bells. They also sent frequent sideways glances at Burke, which made my blood boil. I knew exactly what they were up to. Of course, they probably hadn't come into Shop 'n' Save just to flirt with Burke Walters. But he did happen to be one of the most popular guys at school. And now that they had the chance, I was pretty sure those two wouldn't pass it up.

I was right. The minute Burke pulled their basket up to his register, they were on. I couldn't hear them all the time, but I didn't need to. Body language says a lot. The conversation went something like this:

Lydia and Marci: Hi, Burke. (They giggle)

Burke: Hi, Lydia. Marci.

Lydia: Working hard today?

Burke: I always do.

I held my breath. The crucial moment had come. Would he play along with them? Would he flirt back? Would there be that awful, sickening gleam in his eyes that guys usually got around Lydia and Marci?

I chewed on my thumbnail.

"Psst!" came a hiss through the tunnel. "Allie, are you watching?"

"Of course I am!" I hissed back.

"He hasn't even looked at her!" Nicky noted gleefully.

"I know, but—"

Right at that moment Lydia leaned over the checkout counter toward Burke. And I mean *leaned.* My view of her face was blocked by the produce scales, but I could see Marci clearly. She was smiling like a cat. Burke's expression remained completely blank. I watched in horror as Lydia lifted a forefinger and touched his nose.

Nicky's gasp came through the tunnel like steam from an iron. "Of all the nerve!"

I was too mortified to speak. *Oh, please,* I prayed in a mental message to Burke, *please let me take good news back to Marion.*

As if in answer, Burke jerked away from Lydia's finger. His expression came into clear view when he turned back to his cash register. There was no sparkle in his eyes. He simply went about his business, leaving Lydia in the lurch.

I felt like cheering. Nicky did more than feel like it. Her voice rose way above a whisper.

"Did you see that?" she asked. "Wasn't it terrific?"

"Yeah," I agreed. "But let's keep it down, OK?"

She didn't seem to hear me. And I couldn't see her through the tunnel anymore. When I finally did see her again, the look in her eyes had changed to terror. The look in mine was probably the same because all of a sudden I had sensed the boxes around me shaking. I had been in California earthquakes before, and the feeling was similar—but not quite the same. All the shaking was concentrated in one area, right in front of my nose. Dozens of Crunch-O cereal boxes were trembling as if they had lives of their own.

The last I saw of Nicky's face was the startled expression in her blue eyes. Then the tunnel collapsed, and I felt the first bonk on my head. After that came a steady stream of cardboard.

Chapter Six

Cereal boxes are not very heavy. But if they fall one right after the other, the person whose head they are landing on tends to become a little rattled. That's why it took me about half a minute to understand what was going on. By then I was standing in a pile of Crunch-O boxes, the display in ruins. And the worst yet to come.

"Hey, Allie, are you all right?"

I lowered my arms, which I'd raised over my head to shield me from the avalanche. Then, slowly, I turned and saw Burke. Beside him stood a tall woman in a white-and-green Shop 'n' Save smock. They both stared at me as though I'd been struck by lightning. I guess I must have looked that way—eyes wide, mouth open, speechless. My cheeks must have been flaming red, too. I was beginning to feel about as embarrassed as I had ever felt in my life.

The embarrassment got even worse when I remembered Nicky and looked around for her. Between us lay a giant mess. And around us stood about a dozen people, some frowning, some grinning. Many were *trying* not to laugh.

"I'm terribly sorry, girls," the woman in the smock said. "I had no idea this display was so unstable. Would you like to come sit down in my office for a while?"

Suddenly I realized that this woman was worried about us and that she was the manager of the store. Instead of getting yelled at, Nicky and I were being apologized to.

I found my voice. "I think—we're OK. Thank you. It was just, um, kind of surprising."

This caused a whole new burst of laughter from our audience. Burke stepped up and took my arm in one hand, guiding me around the wreckage to Nicky. After taking her arm, too, he led us both away.

"Oh, no," Marion moaned.

"Mare," I said softly. "Just listen a minute, OK? Let us explain."

We were all sitting in the cafeteria on Wednesday. Our table was in the corner so if anyone came around to eavesdrop, we'd be sure to notice.

Marion just shook her head. "I think I've heard enough."

"No, wait. It wasn't that bad," I insisted. "After Burke took us to the water fountain, he just asked if we were sure we were all right."

"And get this," Nicky added. "He said that the guy who had set up that display really didn't know what he was doing. Can you believe it?" She slapped her knee and laughed. "He was really apologetic."

Marion glared at her. "This is funny? You terrorize a whole grocery store, wreck the merchandise, cause trouble for *my* boyfriend—"

"Whoa!" I interrupted. "We did not cause Burke trouble. No one, including Burke, had the slightest idea that we had been spying."

"Yeah, and we didn't wreck the merchandise, either," Nicky protested, lower lip thrust out. "The boxes just fell. They didn't break open or anything. All the store had to do was stack them back up again."

"The store! *You* should have done that," Marion snapped. "You're the ones who knocked them down."

Nicky's face fell. "But, Marion, it really wasn't our fault. I mean, I may have bumped into it a little, but anyone could have done the same thing. Really, Burke said so himself. It could have fallen on a little old lady instead."

Marion was not convinced. She rolled her eyes.

Sara, who had just been listening until then, leaned forward. "This story is very funny, but incomplete. What about the mission?"

"The mission?" Nicky asked.

"In other words, did you learn anything?"

I snapped my fingers. "Oh, the mission! You're right. We did learn something. Something wonderful, Marion!"

As we described Burke's cold reaction to Lydia's flirting, Marion's expression began to change. From frowning and superior, it turned relieved. Then she caught herself and tried to hide her little smile.

"Well, what did you expect?" She shrugged. "That Lydia Marshall really isn't worth anyone's time."

Her voice sounded nonchalant, but I knew Marion too well to be fooled. Under her cool, casual pose, she was relieved. Knowing that I had helped give her that feeling made everything, including the avalanche of Crunch-Os, worthwhile.

To my father, cooking is just about the ultimate in fun. I get to experience this questionable joy of cooking on Mondays and Fridays. On Wednesdays and Saturdays I do the dishes, and I'm responsible for the laundry for the last week of every month. The system works out great, as far as I'm concerned, in spite of the cooking part. No one has to do the same chore all the time, and we're not allowed to criticize how anyone does his or her job. One good thing about the cooking part, then, is that you can make the most awful disaster, and no one says a word. You can also make things that you really like, even if they aren't everyone else's favorite. Tempting as it is, I do not often use this power to torture Jake.

Sometimes, though, he deserves it. One of those times came up on Wednesday night.

"Careful, Allie," he warned as I put away some spice jars after dinner. Seated with our parents at the table, he lingered over a piece of especially delicious pie our dad had made.

I glanced over my shoulder. "Careful with what?"

"That cupboard," he said, not looking up. "There are a couple of cereal boxes in there, you know."

My mouth dropped open.

"I mean, those cereal boxes," he went on,

shaking his head. "You never know about them, right?"

Mom and Dad both stared at him oddly. For my part, I was trying to figure out how on earth Jake had heard about the Crunch-O catastrophe.

"This must be an inside joke," Mom said.

"Guess you could say so," Jake answered. "But I'll fill you in. It seems that your darling daughter here, with the help of one of her weird friends, managed to knock over about a hundred boxes of cereal at Shop 'n' Save yesterday."

Three pairs of eyes focused on me. I felt so embarrassed I could have climbed into the cupboard to hide. What would my parents think of me? I was also furious at Jake for telling. And I was dying to know how he had found out about the whole disaster in the first place. At least Marion had talked us out of keeping a log book. I hated to imagine the fun Jake would have had discovering that!

"Lydia Marshall told a bunch of us all about it today at lunch," he said, in answer to my unspoken question.

"How," my dad asked in a tone of voice that I didn't quite understand, "did this happen, Allie?"

I looked from him to my mother—avoiding

looking at Jake, who I knew was grinning from ear to ear—and shrugged. "We just kind of bumped into it."

"You bumped into it?" my mom repeated.

I nodded. "Nicky did. But everyone said that it wasn't our fault. I mean, the store manager herself apologized to us. And Burke said the display hadn't been set up right in the first place, and—"

"It *all* fell down?" My mother held one set of knuckles pressed against her lips. For a moment I thought she was feeling sorry for me—sympathizing and fretting that her own baby daughter might have gotten hurt by all those boxes. I was wrong. Mom's eyes suddenly lit up. She was the first to burst out laughing. Dad followed. And before I could say another word, my family was in stitches, at my expense.

Cruel, I thought. *I have a cruel brother and insensitive parents.*

I did, for a moment, feel relieved that at least my folks weren't mad. And at least they weren't going to grill me for further details. But soon, indignation welled up. "I'm glad," I told them angrily, "that you're all enjoying yourselves."

Mom bit her lip, and Dad covered his mouth, but they couldn't stop laughing. It was a wonder I heard the phone ring over all their racket. On the way to answer it, I decided if the caller was one of Jake's friends, I'd tell him about some embarrassing thing Jake had once done. When I picked it up, I was all prepared to say, "Hi, there. Did you know that Jake once ran out into the street in nothing but his underwear because he dreamed the house was on fire?" But I didn't have a chance to do any such thing. The sound of Greg's voice on the line stopped me. I couldn't utter a word after saying hello.

"Um, may I speak with Allie, please?"

"This is she," I said, finally coaxing my vocal cords back to life. "Hi, Greg!"

"Oh, hi. Sorry, I didn't recognize your voice. How's it going?"

"Fine." *Wonderful!* I wanted to say. *Now that you're calling me!* For privacy, I dragged the phone out of the kitchen into the hallway. My heart was pounding so hard I thought I'd better find a place to sit. I sank to the carpet.

"Played any more Missile Command lately?" he asked.

"No, not since Saturday. I guess school's been keeping me busy this week."

"Yeah," he said. "Me, too. Have you started on that history project yet?"

So that was it. He was calling about school.

My racing heart began to settle down. It was just an ordinary call about homework. No big deal.

"No," I answered. "Not yet. How about you?"

"Yeah, sort of. I've been looking at this guide sheet he gave us. You know, the tough part is going to be choosing a topic. Once you get that, it won't be so bad."

In a strange sort of way, I felt relieved. Greg and I were still just friends. Nothing new or risky. But on the other hand, I was terribly disappointed. If only Saturday night had changed things between us!

During our whole conversation about history class and school in general, there was no sign of any such change. Greg never even asked me a specific question about the assignment. I couldn't figure out why, exactly, he had called. But for about ten minutes I enjoyed just listening to his voice. Our talk could probably have gone on forever if it hadn't been for my dear brother.

"Hey!" he yelled from the kitchen. "Don't be afraid to come back in here and finish cleaning up, Allie. The cereal boxes are all safely put away."

My stomach dropped. Desperately, I hoped Greg hadn't heard about my adventure with Nicky.

Jake's yelling roused my mother, too. "Oh, yes, honey, and I'm expecting a call. Don't stay on too long."

I could have throttled Jake.

"I guess I have to get going now," I said, sighing.

"Oh, sure. I hope I haven't kept you too long," Greg's voice was really apologetic, as if I'd done him a big favor by talking with him.

"Not at all, Greg, really," I said. "I mean—if you ever have any questions about history or anything—" I felt so stupid. Why couldn't I just come out and say I'd like to hear from him again?

"OK, well, thanks."

"Sure," I mumbled.

"Well, um, see you in class tomorrow?"

"Yeah."

This was it. The end. He would hang up, we'd talk the next day at school, and that would be that. No moonlit walks together, no nightly calls, no romantic outings. Things would drag along as always. Unless—

"Yes?" He didn't exactly sound disappointed that I was continuing the conversation.

"Um, would you be interested in maybe— playing some more video games or something this weekend?"

Silence. My entire nervous system teetered on the brink of panic.

"This weekend? Sure, Allie, that sounds great!"

It took a minute for his enthusiasm to sink in. I could hardly believe how happy he sounded.

"I'd really like that a lot," he went on. "Or how about if we see a movie? Or go have some dinner somewhere?"

"Allie," Jake hollered. "Mom's expecting a call."

Brothers have wonderful timing.

"Yeah, Greg. That sounds terrific. But I have to go, now. We can talk in class tomorrow, OK?"

"Great. I, um, I'll see you, Allie."

I clung to the phone for a second after his final click. Then I set it down as if it were a beautiful, fragile work of art.

Chapter Seven

My friends could not get over the fact that I had asked Greg out. At lunchtime, after he and I had settled the details about our date, I gave them the whole story.

"You just came out and *asked* him?" Marion wondered. "Just like that?"

I shrugged. "Guess so."

"Hey, don't give her such a hard time," Nicky said. "Why shouldn't Allie have asked a boy out? This *isn't* the nineteenth century, you know."

She was the only one who didn't gape at my news. That was a bit ironic. Nicky had so many dates, she would never have to ask a boy out.

"But weren't you afraid that he'd say no?" Sara asked.

I took a bite out of my sandwich. "If I had stopped to think about it, I suppose I would have been. But I guess I didn't have a chance to."

"Hmmm." Sara studied a swirl in her mashed potatoes. "My sister would approve. She says it's not fair for girls to have to sit and wait to be chosen, and that it's also not fair for guys to have to carry the full risk of rejection."

Marion nodded. "Rejection. That's the tough part. Let's say you ask a boy out, and he says yes just to be nice. The way girls do sometimes. Then, after the date, he doesn't call you or anything. What do you do?"

"Ask him out again," Nicky suggested. "Don't be so negative, Marion. Allie's not going to have that problem. From the looks Sara saw him giving her, I think Greg really likes her."

Her words made me tingle. "You really think so?" I asked.

"Oh, absolutely! Don't you let these two old worriers get you all upset about going out with Greg. According to you three, I'm supposed to be the expert on boys, right? Well, then, my official opinion is that Allie Perrin-James and Greg Segura are going to have a terrific time together!"

For the rest of the week, I clung to Nicky's prediction. Neither Greg nor I drove yet, so our parents drove us to the restaurant we had chosen. Greg walked up to our car Saturday night as soon as we pulled into the parking lot. Right away, he introduced himself to my father. My heart swelled with pride. His manner was a little bit shy, as usual, but he smiled and shook hands and looked absolutely wonderful. After giving my dad a peck boodbye, I was finally on my own with Greg. What a feeling! As soon as we got to the sidewalk in front of the tiny El Faro restaurant, he took my hand.

"You look great," he said, gazing at me. "I like your sweater. That blue looks really nice on you."

His eyes were warm and friendly. My stomach did a flip. *Dear, sweet Nicky,* I thought, *you were right. Greg does like me.* And he really looked happy that I'd asked him out.

"Thanks," I answered. "I like your sweater, too." It was the one with the little fleet of reindeer on it. I decided I would never look at Santa's sleigh in quite the same way again.

"Well," Greg said when we reached the door, "you ready for a taco terrifico? Or a burstin' burrito?"

"You bet!"

The host seated us at a little wooden table for two right next to the homemade fountain that made El Faro look like a real Mexican patio garden. Really the place was just a hole-in-the-wall, but the family who owned it had taken pains to make it look as authentic as possible.

"Wonder who takes care of all these plants," Greg mused.

Lit by strings of colored lights, the restaurant was a jungle of ferns and vines.

"Maybe they fertilize them with Mexican food," I suggested. "It's good enough to make anything grow."

Greg laughed, and that was how our conversation got started. I mentioned that my dad had just gotten a tortilla-making kit for his cooking studio. Greg asked about the studio, so I had to go into the whole explanation about my dad's profession.

"Wow," Greg exclaimed. "You mean he's a chef?"

I shook my head. "Not exactly. He calls himself a professional cook. I guess there's a difference. Anyway, he runs this cooking school downtown, and people come from miles around for lessons."

Greg still looked a little amazed, but I wasn't offended at all. I was accustomed to seeing people in various stages of surprise over my dad's career.

"But he's so—"

"Big?" I finished for him. That was another common response. "Yes, he is. He played football in college, but just for the scholarship money. He's not at his best until he ties on his apron."

Greg laughed. "Wow, that's great. I mean, he must have guts."

"Guts?"

"Well, yeah. Even nowadays guys are expected to do things like play football or be firemen or lawyers or something. Your dad must have had to stand up to some pressure— other guys making fun of him."

"Oh, he'd just ignore it if they did," I said, shrugging. "I think he'd rather be stuffing ravioli than defending his reputation."

Greg laughed again, but even as we joked around, I was glad he'd said that about my father. It was nice to know that he could accept, and even admire, my unusual father. A little bit later he asked about my last name, too. When I explained that it's half my mom's name and half my dad's, he said he thought that was great. Kevin Neville had thought it was the weirdest thing since dried figs. It didn't help much when I explained to Kevin that some women don't change their names when they marry. Some, like my mom, want their kids to share their names, too. Kevin didn't understand. I felt happier than ever to be with Greg.

After dinner we went to see a movie—not a monster flick—and he didn't even try to sit too close to the screen. In fact, everything went perfectly until after the movie.

I left Greg in the lobby and went to the ladies' room, which turned out to be quite a mistake. As soon as I swung through the door, I heard high, bell-like laughter. There stood Marci and Lydia, brushing their hair.

I suppressed a groan. The last people I wanted to see were the ones who had broadcast the Crunch-O disaster all over Lomitas High. But it was so crowded that there was a chance they'd never see me. *I'll just sneak in and sneak out,* I thought. Not a chance.

"Hi, Allie," Lydia cooed.

"Hi," I mumbled back. I had to practically bite my tongue to keep from asking if she had any more good gossip about me. It would have felt great to tell her off, but Nicky and I had made fools of ourselves in a public place, and anyone had a right to talk about it.

I ducked into a stall and tried to put the blabbermouths out of my mind. But hard as I tried, I couldn't shut out their voices. Most of what they said was easy to ignore. But then, just as I was coming out of the stall, I heard one name that made me stop and listen. *Paul Danberg*. I strained to hear more over the din of other voices. What business did Lydia and Marci have discussing the guy Sara was interested in?

"He's out there," Lydia said, giggling.

In response, Marci said something that I didn't catch. I took my time washing my hands.

"I know he'll be glad to see you, Marci," Lydia went on.

My heart sank. Lydia was guiding Marci in a chase after Paul? *Rats! Poor Sara.*

On their way out, they swept past me and uttered two sweet little goodbyes. My response came out as a semigrunt. It wasn't that I really had anything against them. I mean, I'm not the type who dislikes other girls because of their looks or popularity. But of all the guys at Lomitas, why did Marci have to pick Paul?

Feeling totally crestfallen, I finished combing my hair. How could Sara compete with a blond bombshell like Marci? As I put my comb away, though, a glimmer of hope came over me. Maybe Paul's response to Marci would be the same as Burke's had been to Lydia. Why should I assume he'd fall for her? I rushed out of the bathroom, anxious to witness the scene.

But as I stepped back into the lobby, another thought hit me. What was I doing? How could I spy while I was on the date I had dreamed about for weeks? How crazy could I get?

I looked around for Greg. It would be nice to be back by his side, my hand in his. Just as I'd imagined it, we would stroll down Shepherd Avenue—alone, this time—and smile and laugh and gaze into each other's eyes. But all that could not take place until I found him, and he was nowhere in sight.

I didn't worry. Most likely he had gone into the restroom himself and would be out any minute. While I waited, I decided to get a drink at the water fountain. That turned out to be my second mistake for the evening.

At first I didn't see them. So much for alertness. But as I bent over for a sip, I caught a flash of blond out of the corner of my eye. When I looked a little closer, I saw none other than Marci and Paul and Lydia standing in a cozy little group at the popcorn stand.

Right away I wished I hadn't been thirsty. The look on Paul's face and the way he kept leaning close to Marci made me sick. His response to the Devastating Duo was very different from Burke's.

I knew it didn't make sense to be mad at the three of them, but I couldn't help myself. Paul should have been saving his smiles for Sara!

"There you are."

The voice in my ear and the hand on my shoulder made me jump about ten feet.

"Where've you been?" Greg asked.

I just stared at him for a second, still in a daze over what I had seen. Then I recovered and said, "Oh, I just, um, came over to get a drink of water."

His frown relaxed a little. "I was waiting for you over by the exit until I realized that the big fake palm tree might be hiding me."

"Oh, maybe it did. I didn't see you."

He smiled. "Well, I'm glad I found you."

The way he said it made me think of all kinds of wonderful, romantic things. For a moment I forgot all about that creep Paul and the way he had looked at Marci. But that was just for a moment. Before we'd even reached the sidewalk, my mind was doing an instant replay of the whole scene. It made me feel just awful for Sara.

We had walked about halfway back to El Faro, where I was to meet my dad, before I realized that Greg knew something was bothering me. He ambled silently beside me, his hands in his pockets. This was not turning out to be the romantic stroll I'd had in mind.

"Hmmm, nice night, huh?" I asked, trying to bridge the gap between us.

"Oh, yeah. Beautiful." He gazed up into the heavens, then turned his eyes to me.

I smiled. "I've really enjoyed tonight, Greg."

His responding smile was all the answer I needed. "I'm really glad you suggested it."

My heart thumped. "Really?"

"Sure." Suddenly he stopped walking. "I really like being with you, Allie."

I looked down, afraid that if I kept my eyes on his face I'd turn into a lump of mush. "Thanks."

He took my hand then, and we kept walking. That night, I knew, there wouldn't be much chance for the heart-stopping good night kiss I'd imagined. Our parents would be waiting for us at the restaurant. But I smiled, relieved that our little romantic stroll had gotten back on track. I was determined that Marci's flirting with the boy of my best friend's dreams would not ruin my first night out with the boy of *my* dreams.

Chapter Eight

"See? Didn't I tell you?" Nicky crowed into the phone so loud that I had to hold the receiver away from my ear.

"Greg's crazy about you, and you had a wonderful time together last night, just like I said you would!"

"Well, we did have a wonderful time," I agreed.

"*And* he's crazy about you," she insisted. "When are you going out again?"

I paused. "We didn't really talk about it." For a moment I got worried. Greg hadn't brought up the subject of another date. Did that mean he wasn't interested in one?

Nicky was unflappable. "Well, no matter. You will."

It was nice to have such an optimistic

friend. The world could be coming to an end, and Nicky Gould would remark on the lovely weather. Marion, on the other hand, would have already spent several weeks predicting the catastrophe, and Sara would engross herself in a gloomy scientific analysis of it.

The thought of Sara reminded me of why I had called Nicky in the first place.

"I've got a question for you," I said, preparing her for the inevitable bad news. "Um, remember how when Lydia Marshall came on to Burke, he ignored her." Nicky said she did. "OK, what if you saw her and Marci walk up to another guy, pull the same tricks, and *not* get ignored?"

"Hmmm," Nicky mused. "You mean, get paid attention to? Encouraged, even?"

"Right."

"Maybe it depends on the guy you're talking about. But usually—"

"It means bad news," I finished for her.

"Exactly. Why? Which guy *are* you talking about?"

"Oh, just one of the few we would least want to see flirting with Marci McDonald. A guy one of us happens to be nuts about."

"Greg?" Nicky asked in horror.

"No!" I roared, about ten times more horrified.

"Well, it couldn't be Burke. Hmm. Oh, no, not Paul!"

"You got it," I confirmed.

Nicky groaned. She was probably thinking the same thing I was—of all the guys for Marci to set her sights on.

"Well, are you sure he looked interested?" she asked.

"Positive. That might not have worried me too much, but I overheard Lydia and Marci plotting about Paul. They just couldn't wait to go after him. And they *didn't* wait, either."

"Oh, great. Just great," she said. "Once those two launch a campaign to get a guy, they don't give up easily. And if Paul encouraged them, Sara's in for some big trouble."

I started biting a nail. What Nicky wasn't saying, but probably meant, was that Sara wouldn't have a chance against Marci. The thought cut me to the quick. Sara was a lovely, wonderful person. But I wasn't sure she could muster the kind of feminine charm that Marci had been cultivating for years.

There was no way around it. With Marci as competition, Sara was in for one big heartbreak.

"There must be something we can do," I heard myself mumbling.

"Something we can do?" Nicky repeated.

"Like what, for pete's sake? Find Marci another target?"

I snorted. "Hardly. But—" Suddenly I had a great idea. At least it seemed great. It must have hit Nicky at just the same time because she nearly broke my eardrum again.

"Hey, we'll find *Sara* another target!" she shrieked.

As soon as my ear had recovered, I put the phone back up to it. "Yeah! Exactly what I was thinking. But the problem is—"

"The problem is *who*?" Nicky finished. "Actually, that's not such a problem. You just leave the who to me. When I find him, the problem will be Sara."

I agreed. Getting Sara's attention away from Paul would be no easy task.

"I'll do some scouting around," Nicky assured me. "Don't worry. I'll find someone just perfect!"

I did worry. Nicky and I didn't discuss the matter again that week, because Sara was with us most of the time. We were all also pretty busy with homework. By Saturday, though, Sara was on my mind again.

I sat in the front office of my dad's cooking school, typing up a stack of student information cards. It was not exactly the most fascinating of tasks. Typing card after card listing name, address, phone number, and interests was pretty boring. I still found it hard to believe that so many otherwise intelligent people wanted to pay good money just to learn how to put together a few simple meals. But some of dad's students had been coming to classes ever since he and his partners opened Quintessential Cuisine three years before. Mrs. Rimlinger, for instance, talked about copper pans the way some people talk about religion.

But then again, my friends and I talked about boys as much as Dad's students talked about food. I sighed. Why *did* we think about boys so much? I, for one, had been pretty happy that week. Things with Greg had been going great. I smiled, thinking about how in less than one hour he'd be coming by to meet me. But what about poor Sara? She had mentioned Paul to me at least three different times that week. As smart as she was, she was spending too much time thinking about a creep of a guy who would probably never even look at her twice. And as for our plan to find her a substitute—well, I had my doubts.

If only I could find a way to be honest with Sara, to tell her what I hd seen. "He's a no-good nothing," I wanted to say, "who knows no better than to flirt with an airhead like Marci."

But how could I say such a thing? It would floor her!

I sighed again, typing the twenty-second zip code onto the twenty-second information card. Maybe if the work weren't so terribly boring, I thought, my mind wouldn't wander to such depressing subjects as Sara's love life. Sometimes I wished Dad would let me help him teach his classes. I could chop carrots and stir the sauce or something. But then again, that would probably be even more boring than typing zip codes. I looked through the glass wall that separated the office from the kitchen. Beyond it stood eight grown men and women sautéing mushrooms. I quickly decided to stick to typing.

With a glance at the clock, I saw that I had only another few minutes before I'd get to see Greg. We had planned a walk in the park, with maybe a stop for a sandwich. To my surprise, it seemed very natural to plan an afternoon like that.

Even though we hadn't had much time alone on our first date, I still felt a tingling rush when I thought about our holding hands. And during the past week at school, we acted as if we shared some terrific secret. I still listened to Ms. Kubiesky in history class, but the whole time I could sense Greg's nearness. And I flushed with happiness whenever he looked at me.

Those last minutes in my dad's office flew by. Mercifully, I only made a couple of mistakes on the student cards. I heard the little tinkle of the bell tied to the top of the door, and in walked Greg.

"Hi!" His eyes lingered on me. "I almost didn't find you. I walked by the building twice before I saw the entrance."

I smiled. "Yeah, I should have warned you. My dad and his partners don't believe in big flashy signs. They like to keep the entrance homey."

That word did not apply to the inside of the school. I watched Greg to see what his reaction would be to all the sleek, high-tech equipment and modern furniture. My dad certainly didn't run a sunny country kitchen. There were no ceramic roosters or gingham curtains in sight. Not even a potted plant. Everything from the walls to the smallest saucer was either black, white, chrome, or glass. The effect was most austere and impressive.

"Wow, this is a really neat place," Greg commented.

"Pretty nice," I agreed.

"So this is where he teaches, huh?" he asked, pointing through the window. "A class in progress?"

I nodded. "Yup. My father at work."

For a little while we stood and watched the students mix a sauce, with my father peering over their shoulders to offer advice.

"Hmmm." Greg narrowed his eyes. "Who gets to eat all the stuff they cook in there?"

"They do, mostly. But it isn't always good, you know."

"Well," he began hopefully, "maybe they need some tester tastebuds like mine. Think I could get a job?"

I laughed. "I don't know, but my dad did say he'd be happy to give you a tour of the kitchen sometime when he isn't teaching a class."

"That's a start." Greg licked his lips and patted his belly.

We talked more about the cooking school on the way to the park. I explained that my father had been a miserable insurance salesman before a couple of friends convinced him to give it up and do what he really liked. So he went to study in Paris, met my mom at a sidewalk cafe, and then came back home with her to live happily ever after.

"Pretty romantic," Greg said, smiling. "And I thought *my* family was different!"

"Why?" I asked. "Does your dad do something as weird as mine does?"

He shook his head. "Afraid not. He's a professor over at the college."

"Really? Wow! What does he teach?"

"Anthropology. He specializes in Latin America," Greg explained. "He's originally from Mexico."

"Oh, so that's where you get your eyes." I gazed at him, wanting to mention how big and soft and gorgeous I thought his eyes were. I loved the striking contrast between them and his auburn hair. But I didn't, though.

"How about your mom?" I ended up asking. "Is she from Mexico, too?"

Greg smiled. "Nope. Her side is Scotch-Irish. That's where I got this reddish hair." He tugged on a lock of hair.

"And I'll bet that's where you got those, too," I said, pointing to the sprinkle of freckles across his nose.

He turned and gave me such a warm, caring look that my knees went wobbly. Then he gently wrapped his fingers around mine. "Guess so," he replied.

Somehow, I managed to keep walking.

"Do you want to be a college professor, too?" I asked, gradually regaining some steadiness.

"I don't know if I could get into grading

papers all the time, the way profs have to. But I do like anthropology, and archeology, too. That's what my mother is—an archeologist. I wouldn't mind doing what she does, excavating ancient tombs and stuff."

"Really? That sounds interesting," I told him.

"Yeah, except that she teaches most of the time, too. Our house is usually one big mountain of ungraded exams and term papers." He didn't seem to mind, though. "What do you think you want to do? Would you ever want to take over your dad's cooking school?"

"No way!" I shook my head.

Greg laughed.

"Maybe I'll—" I clamped my mouth shut, stopping just short of saying, "become a spy."

Aside from the obvious reason, I stopped myself because spying wasn't really what I wanted to do. True, I did want some adventure in my life, and maybe I'd think about being a private eye or police detective. But I'd never really became a spy. I didn't want *that* much adventure. Sara and Marion and Nicky just liked to tease me about the CIA and the FBI, but they knew I wasn't serious.

He looked at me oddly. "You'll what?"

"Oh, I guess I'll have to think about it."

He nodded. "At least there's plenty of time

for that." Then he squeezed my hand and gave me another one of those melting gazes.

I suppose that if I had been used to boys looking at me that way, I simply would have looked back at him. Maybe I would have even leaned over and kissed him.

But I wasn't the least bit used to getting admiring, meaningful glances from boys. As a kind of defense against my own nervousness, I started to act silly.

First I pointed out the big flock of ducks quacking all over the pond. Then I pulled him over to the pond and pretended to throw bread into the water so that the ducks would come to shore. They did, and before I knew it, we were surrounded by a quacking, waddling mass.

"Guess they're hungry," Greg observed.

"*How* hungry?" Ducks had never seemed particularly threatening to me before, but then again I had never been surrounded by dozens of them.

"Here," Greg offered, tugging me toward a big rock a few feet away. "Refuge."

We climbed up and found a perfect spot in the sun.

"Excellent," I said. "From here we can look down upon our little feathered friends."

"They were pretty friendly, weren't they?" he asked, grinning.

We laughed and started tossing pebbles out onto the pond's cool green surface. That excited the ducks into paddling back out.

"They can't be that hungry," I protested. "This pond is stocked with fish. I've come out here before and watched them dive down for dinner."

"Maybe they like bread crusts better," Greg suggested and tossed another pebble.

I wrapped my arms around my knees, face up to the sun. We weren't holding hands anymore, but I still felt very close to and comfortable with Greg up there on our private rock. If he did look at me again in that special way, I decided, I would not freak out and start acting silly. Instead, I would nestle in his arms. I would delight in the touch of his lips on mine, and—

"Allie," he said suddenly, startling me out of my daydream.

"Yes?"

He was still tossing pebbles, one after the other, farther and farther out. The ducks had lost interest.

"When I was a kid," he began, his eyes on the water, "sometimes when I made friends, I'd get jealous if they played with anyone else. I was pretty possessive, I guess. Maybe it was because I'm an only child and I wasn't really used to playing with other kids. I've gotten over that now, but—well—I've never had a girlfriend before, and—"

My heart began to thump.

"I wonder if maybe I did try to hold on to you too tight," he said, tossing in another pebble. "I mean, would that put you off?"

He wouldn't look at me, but I couldn't take my eyes off him. I also couldn't get a word out because I was so surprised.

Finally I managed to say, "No. I—I wouldn't feel that way at all."

"Are you sure?" He turned to me with a concerned, searching look on his face.

"Very sure," I answered softly.

The sun streamed down on us, warming my back. It sparkled off the surface of the pond. From a distance we could hear muffled quacks and splashes. Greg and I had been sitting just inches apart from each other, but then it was as if we each had a magnet inside. At almost the same instant we leaned forward. Then, very gently we kissed.

Chapter Nine

"Time flies when you're having fun." I had never believed in that saying. Before that day in March, when Greg and I sat on our rock until the sun set, most of my life had moved slowly. But when Greg Segura came into my life, the hands began to race each other around the clock.

In addition to Greg a lot of other factors went into keeping me busier than ever. And it all seemed to happen at once. To start with, Mom had to go to a conference in Oregon for a week. That meant I had to do more work at home. Then Dad and his partners decided to computerize their business. The computer at school was really fun to play around on, so the word "computerize" to me meant less work and all the information I could want at the touch of a button. At first, I even felt worried that it might beat me out of my Saturday job. Fat chance. In the beginning, at least, I had more work than ever. All the files on paper had to be keyed in on the new terminal. Bye-bye, information cards; hello, print out. I really didn't mind. Dad hired me to work Friday afternoons, too, which meant double my weekly pay. And after a couple of weekends, I had pretty much gotten the hang of the computer's funny whirrs and clicks.

As if all that activity weren't enough to keep me spinning, we also had midterms at school.

And what about Mission: Love? Well, it kind of took a backseat.

"Allie!" Nicky called, catching up with me on the way home one Tuesday after my biology exam. "I found one!"

I was still tired from staying up to study the night before, and so I stared at her, confused. "One what?"

"A guy," she whispered as if I should know. "For Sara."

Those four words were enough to make me feel like a rat. It had been over two weeks since I'd given more than a passing thought to Sara and Paul and Marci. Somehow, now that I was having so much fun with Greg, everyone else's problems had faded away.

"Ted Hawkins. I was walking to my locker, and there he was at his locker. I saw this poster hung up on the inside of it that had some Latin words on it. So I asked him what they said, and he said, 'Knowledge is the Key,' and I just knew he'd be right for Sara!"

Selfish, I chided myself, *that's what you've been*. Sara deserved much more attention than I'd been paying her.

"Ted Hawkins," I said thoughtfully. "He was in my English class last year. He's really smart."

"Oh, yeah," Nicky agreed. "And kind of cute, too, don't you think?"

I nodded. "But I'm not sure he can compete with Paul in Sara's book."

"Oh, but we've just got to give it a try, Allie. I asked Ted how he'd like to go on a double date with me and a friend of mine."

"You did?" My eyes opened wide with admiration.

Nicky shrugged, as if there was nothing to on-the-spot matchmaking. "He asked me who, and I said Sara Novello, and he said, 'Sure, why not.' "

Leave it to Nicky.

"You'll talk to Sara, right?" she pleaded.

I sighed. "Give me the easy part, huh?" Even as I complained, I knew inside it was my duty to help set things right for Sara. I wasn't the kind of person who would turn my back on a friend in need, just because things happened to be going well for me.

That line of thinking led me straight into trouble.

After Nicky took off for lunch, I headed for the library in search of Sara. During midterms, that was where she spent every free moment, including lunchtime.

As I entered the big, airy room, I smiled and nodded to Mr. Loftis, the librarian. The high ceilings, skylights, and big potted palms made it easy to see why Sara liked studying there. But at this time in the semester, the place was so crowded that I wondered how she could concentrate.

Apparently she had had the same doubts. She wasn't at any of the worktables, or in the carrels, or in the closed-off conference rooms at the back. After giving one last look through the stacks, I figured she had gone to lunch after all.

I turned back through the stacks, busily figuring out how to convince Sara that Ted could be the new love of her life. He's cute, I'd say. And intelligent, interesting, and available.

It's possible that I never would have noticed

Bob and Dennis sitting at a table nearby if Dennis hadn't suddenly let out a laugh so loud and rollicking that the ever-tolerant Mr. Loftis was forced to ask him to be quiet. Chances were, also, that I would have kept on walking if it hadn't been for the nagging sense of guilt left over from my conversation with Nicky earlier. Hadn't I deserted my friends recently? Sure, I'd helped Marion a little. And the information I'd gotten on Paul might eventually save Sara from a broken heart. But what about Nicky? We hadn't done a thing to settle her doubts about what boys really thought of her. Mission: Love had just faded away, and I had let it.

But it's time for lunch, a little voice in me protested. *You can't do this. Oh, yes, I can.*

I ducked behind a stack of books and perked up my ears.

At first I couldn't hear anything from Bob and Dennis's table clearly. All I could gather was that they weren't talking about homework. That gave me some encouragement, at least. I crept farther up along the row of books, until I was on the very end. When I peeked out from behind the shelves in the vain hope of reading their lips, I noticed something too lucky to ignore. The table they occupied stood a good fifteen feet away from me. But right next to it, between us, there was an empty table. It was just waiting for me.

It took about six seconds to make up my mind. I glanced to the left, and then to the right. I checked Mr. Loftis and then my targets. They did not appear to be on guard against a girl crawling out of the stacks to spy on them. In another thirty seconds, I had dashed out from behind the bookshelves and scrambled under the table.

You, the little voice told me, *are crazy. Wouldn't it be just wonderful if Greg saw you?*

I ignored the little voice. What will be will be. It was too late to change my mind, anyway. I was already crouched down under a library table with Bob and Dennis just a couple of yards away.

I didn't think anyone could see me because the table was near the back of the library. Also, six big wooden chairs stood around me like a shield. If I could manage to keep quiet and not bump into any of them as I crawled, everything would be OK.

Everything *was* OK for a while. On my hands and knees I made it about three-quarters of the way down the length of the table. Going any farther, I figured, would make it pretty easy for Bob or Dennis to glance down and spot me. But I didn't need to go farther. Right where I was, I could hear almost every word that passed between them.

Although they kept their voices low, it all came through clearly. I felt successful even though their conversation had nothing at all to do with Nicky. If I could just wait long enough, I told myself, her name was bound to come up. They must talk about her plenty, considering how much time they spent chasing her.

My knees, though, were not interested in waiting. Neither was my hunched-over back or my elbows, which were not used to supporting half my body weight. Before long my whole body began to cry out for relief. It did not understand the concepts of friendship and duty.

When Bob and Dennis started talking about cars, my joints began to ache even more. The concepts of friendship and duty waned in importance. I began to think about getting out. Of course, I would have to crawl backward all the way to the end of the table. There was also the risk of bumping into chair legs and table legs and attracting attention. But I was willing to take those risks. Then I saw the feet. Four of them to be exact. Two were in running shoes, and two were in heels. All of them were coming my way.

"Oh, Len," a high, bell-like voice sang. "Don't be silly."

I knew that voice. I knew those feet, in fact. Who else would wear red patent leather heels with fluorescent orange cropped pants.

One person would, for sure.

"Here, have a seat, Lydia," Len said.

Lydia's latest victim, I thought. Len had been in my Spanish class the year before. He was one of the biggest, noisiest jocks on campus.

Before I could react, he was pulling a chair out from *my* table and offering it to her.

"Thank you," she said and sat down only about a yard from me.

They had chosen seats nearest the book stacks, which very neatly closed off my escape route. To get out, I would have to crawl out right up under Bob and Dennis's noses.

Relax, I chanted to myself, trying to fight the rising panic. This is no big deal. Soon it will be time for fifth period, and everyone will get up and leave. All I have to do, I kept telling my cramped body, is wait. Patience is a virtue.

Patience did not go over big in the knees and elbows department. I shifted around a little to get more comfortable, and tried to occupy myself with Bob and Dennis's conversation. *Might as well*, I thought. But over Lydia's loud chatter, I couldn't hear a thing.

I rolled my eyes, wondering what I'd done to deserve my terrible predicament.

Then I heard a tiny thump on the carpet beside me. I turned and saw a pen lying just inches away from my feet. Every muscle all the way up to my scalp froze as Lydia's dainty little hand came down to retrieve it.

Afterward my sigh was so heavy, it was a miracle no one heard it.

But before I could catch my breath, the pen fell again.

"Oh, drat!" she muttered.

"I'll get it," Len insisted and reached down. Then he stopped.

So did my heart.

"Maybe I shouldn't get it for you," he suddenly said.

Lydia wiggled her feet. "Why not?"

"Because you called me ridiculous."

"I did not," she insisted, giggling. "You big, mean brute. Now you give me my pen, or else I'll—"

"You'll what?" He laughed, and then they began to struggle. Lydia would reach down for the pen, and Len would hold her away, and then the table would shake and she'd reach again.

Any minute I figured Mr. Loftis would come stalking up, and he'd lean over and get the pen and see me hiding and—

"Yeeaaah!"

I had never heard a boy scream so loud.

"There's a foot down there!"

Chapter Ten

I now know that it is not possible to die from embarrassment. If it were, I'd be long gone.

After Len yelled, he grabbed Lydia and pulled her away from the table. They were peering under it at me from a safe distance when Mr. Loftis arrived.

"What," he asked angrily, "is going on here?"

Silently, Len pointed.

And in front of everyone in the library, I crawled out and said, "I was looking for something."

"Like a lost marble?" Dennis asked, chuckling.

The rest of the crowd chuckled with him, but Mr. Loftis clapped his hands and shooed them away.

Len was still breathing kind of heavily, and
Lydia looked a little pale.

"I'm sorry," I mumbled to them.

"What were you looking for, anyway?" Len
asked, frowning.

My mind raced. What could anyone look for
under a library table, for a long period of time,
in silence?

"Um, I—" Everyone stared. I was stuttering
in embarrassment. Finally, the words tum
bled out. "I was looking for my—my pen."

"Your pen?" Lydia repeated.

I flushed crimson. "I saw yours down there
and I thought it was mine."

Len frowned. "Well, you didn't have to be so
sneaky about it."

"Sorry." I shrugged, staring at the floor. "
didn't want—to disturb you."

Bob laughed.

"All right," Mr. Loftis said. "Enough is
enough. Let's just forget this now, shall we?
think we've had plenty of disturbance here
already."

I mumbled another apology. Then, aware of
about fifty pairs of eyes following me, I made
my way out of the room.

Right after the next class, the razzing
began. "Hey, Allie," a guy yelled as soon as
walked into geometry class. "Saw you scare

the daylights out of Len. What'd you do? Jump out from under the table or something?"

I made a face at him and plopped down next to Marion.

Then Tommy Fu, one of Jake's tennis team friends, got into the act. "Yeah, Allie. We'll bring you a broomstick and a witch's hat tomorrow. Then you can really scare Len."

I was not in the mood to be teased.

"What's all this about?" Marion whispered.

I sighed. "Tell you after class."

On our way to the Pit, I told her the whole story. But three more people stopped me in the hall to make what they thought were amusing comments about my ability to frighten people. Tommy and his annoying friend had managed to spread the word using *their* version of the library scene.

When Jake showed up and tried to defend me, I nearly keeled over with shock.

"Yeah, I'm sure none of *you* has ever done anything that made you look foolish!" He drew himself up to his full six-foot height. "And how about you, Tommy. I seem to remember something about pictures in your locker."

In between sticking up for me, he shot me a couple of disgusted, why-do-you-do-such-stupid-things glances. But for the first time in months, I appreciated having a big brother.

Nevertheless, the teasing went on.

Marion had to work pretty hard not to laugh. "You poor thing," she managed to say, patting me on the back.

All the way down the hall I thought about it—the risk, the humiliation, the questions I was bound to get from Greg. Was Mission: Love worth all of that? Somehow, I doubted it. Spying didn't seem like quite as much fun anymore.

Finally we made it to the relative privacy of the Pit.

"I think I have an announcement to make." I pursed my lips.

Marion raised her perfectly plucked eyebrows.

"You were right," I said. "One hundred percent right—about everything. I'm quitting."

"What?" she demanded.

"No more spying."

"Just like that?" she asked. "You're giving up the excitement, the thrills, the chills?"

"Don't rub it in."

Marion gave me an apologetic smile. "I didn't mean to tease you, Allie. I'm sorry. All I meant was that you were *so* into this spying thing. How can you quit so suddenly?"

"I am no longer into it. I'm now out."

"Oh," Marion said. "You know, it's strange. I don't even feel like saying I told you so."

The puzzled look on her face made me smile in spite of myself. "Good," I said. "I don't need to hear it, anyway. I need someone to tell me I won't be hearing fright jokes for the rest of my life."

"You won't. Not for the rest of your *life*, anyway."

"Just till I graduate, right?"

"Allie," Marion said gently, "don't worry about it. You know people like to tease. The important thing is that you are really calling Mission: Love off."

"Well, wouldn't you? It's been a disaster. I guess you were right when you tried to tell me we weren't kids anymore."

Marion frowned. "Wait a minute. Before you come down on yourself so hard, let me remind you of something. Now, I never did approve of all that sneaking around, but I've got to admit that it did accomplish something. You *did* convince me to stop mistrusting Burke."

"I did?"

"Yes. It didn't exactly happen the way you planned, but—"

"What do you mean?" I pressed.

"Well, I sure didn't mind hearing about his

turned-off reaction to Lydia. But what really helped me was just that, well, you forced me to *think* about my suspicions. I got to feeling kind of silly, I guess, after you and Nicky went to all that trouble at Shop 'n' Save just to prove to me something I never should have doubted. I finally realized that the reason Burke seems far away sometimes is that he gets really tired working so hard after school."

"Really?"

She nodded. "So you did help me, Allie. I—Burke is—well—" As she let out a contented sigh, her dark eyes sparkled. "He's just wonderful."

That made me almost forget about the embarrassing situation in the library. But not quite.

"Ooops! There's the bell," she said. "We'd better get to class."

I nodded and followed her out.

Later I told Nicky I wanted to quit Mission: Love. She was entirely sympathetic.

"I," she assured me that day after school, "would not have been able to crawl out from under that table. I think I would have stayed there till everybody went away!"

Sara, on the other hand, was not quite so understanding. "You got caught," she scolded, "because you ignored all the rules.

You had no plan, no partner, no alternate escape route."

"Maybe so," I agreed humbly.

"So you want to just up and *quit*?"

I didn't like the way she emphasized that word, as if I were a deserter.

"Sorry," I said.

She sighed, too. "Well, if you've made up your mind, then I've come to a decision, too."

"You have?" I asked listlessly. "About what?"

"Paul. I'm going to ask him out."

"You're going to *what*?" I exclaimed.

"Well, *you* asked Greg out, didn't you? And, anyway, I think Paul likes me, Allie. He talks to me pretty often in history."

The whole thing was all my fault. I should have told her about Ted earlier. Now it might be too late. *Proceed with caution*, I warned myself. *You are treading on the thin ice of a devoted heart.*

"And at lunch last week," Sara went on, "I saw him looking at me. He smiled!"

I smiled, too, but what I was thinking was poor, poor Sara. She's so trusting. "Well," I began carefully. "I guess you could ask him out. But you know, well—we didn't quite know if we should tell you this, Sara, but—"

"Tell me what?"

"That Ted Hawkins likes you."

It was a little fib. Ted hadn't actually said he liked Sara. He had only agreed to go out with her. Just the tiniest of exaggerations. Still, I felt guilty about it.

"He, um, he told Nicky," I went on.

"Ted Hawkins?"

I nodded. "He's a nice guy, I hear."

"I hardly know him."

"Well, Nicky said she thought about suggesting a double date or something to him."

Sara gazed at me in surprise. I saw the doubt in her eyes, too. It told me that maybe she wasn't that crazy about asking Paul out, after all. Maybe she was scared. I pounced on her hesitation like a fox.

"Seems like a good idea to go out with Ted, you know. I mean, just for fun. And you wouldn't have to ask *him*," I stressed.

Sara chewed on her bottom lip. "Well, he does seem sort of interesting."

"Mmmm-hmmm," I agreed casually. "He's pretty bright, aside from being cute and everything,"

She nodded.

"Well, so how about if Nicky sets it up?" I asked.

She frowned at me, giving me a scare.

Maybe she was getting suspicious. Had I pushed too hard?

But she just nodded. "Might as well give it a try. I suppose I'll need some dating practice to get ready for Paul."

I sighed and crossed my fingers.

The next couple of days went a little more smoothly. Midterm tests were over, so I wasn't studying late anymore. And April blossomed into a beautiful, breezy month. It was just perfect for Greg's birthday, which fell on Thursday. I took him out for ice cream and gave him a key chain with a little brass G on it, to celebrate his getting his driver's license.

"This is terrific!" he said, hugging me. "Thanks, Allie-gator!" Unfortunately, he had picked up my nickname while hanging around my house. Even after a couple of Sunday dinners at his, I hadn't heard his parents call him anything I could tease him about in return. So I just smiled and said, "You're welcome."

A few minutes later, though, on our way home, a little cloud darkened our time.

"Hey, I've been forgetting to ask you," he began. "What's this I hear about your getting caught under a library table?"

I tried to look calm and just shrugged. "Gossip."

He laughed. "Oh, come on. Did you really do it?"

He looked at me, but I avoided his eyes.

"No," I finally said. "I was looking for my pen." And then I managed to change the subject.

The next day I was hurrying along the hallway to gym class when suddenly Burke and one of his football jock friends walked in front of me from a side corridor. Shoving each other and laughing, they didn't notice me.

Before I could say hello or anything, I heard the jock mutter, "Yeah, she's a real fox. You seen her lately."

Burke shook his head. "Not lately. But I will. On Saturday night, at Anne Bainbridge's party."

My heart stopped.

Burke's friend laughed and gave him another comradely shove before they disappeared into the locker room.

"No," I whispered. "No!"

Desperately, I wished I hadn't heard them. Or, at least that I had seen the look on Burke's face. Then I could be more certain of his intentions toward this unnamed foxy girl.

I knew he couldn't be talking about Marion. He had just seen her at lunch. And she wouldn't be at Anne's party because she was going away. Of course, I reminded myself, Burke might be perfectly innocent. All he had said was that he'd be *seeing* the girl, not pursuing her. She might even be his cousin!

I kept walking. Marion had seemed so confident and secure with Burke recently. She was perfectly happy. If she had given up her suspicions, then why shouldn't I?

I tried to put the whole scene out of my mind and forget it had ever happened. But when I got to the door of the girls' locker room, the doubt still nagged at me.

If only I could have heard more.

All the way back down the hall I fought myself. The whole idea was crazy. It was insane. What if I got caught? But Marion needed me. If Burke really was betraying her, she'd be blind to it since I had convinced her he wasn't. It was my responsibility to find out the truth. I didn't want to go back to spying, but I couldn't bear the thought of Marion's being hurt again, either, it would be all my fault.

The hall was empty. Gym had already started—without me, of course—but I didn't care. I felt almost feverish with anticipation. The boys' locker room, I knew, was set up just like the girls'. It had a little vestibule you had to go through before you actually got inside. I could hide there easily, just for a moment, and listen.

Allie! that little inner voice yelled. *You can't do this!*

I lightly put my hand on the door handle. Then I pushed. It opened only a crack. I peered inside and saw no one. I opened the door wider and listened. Not a sound.

I was almost all the way through the outer door. The double doors beyond lay wide open, and I caught a glimpse of a row of lockers. I took a tiny cat step, then another, and was just about to let the door swing shut behind me when laughter rang out from the locker room.

I don't think I've ever moved so fast. In seconds I was back through the door and racing down the hall, heart pounding like a jackhammer.

Allie, you are nuts!

I took a deep breath and hurried into the girls' locker room, amazed at the risk I had been about to take. What a close call! How would I have explained my way out of that one?

The strangest thing, though, was that even as I thought about how crazy I had been to try to spy on the boys' locker room, I couldn't get Burke's words out of my head.

On Saturday morning I called Sara. She'd be able to help me decide what to do, I thought. Of the four of us, she was probably the most levelheaded, the one who could see things in perspective. Sara would not get too emotional.

"Ted is gross!" she wailed as soon as she realized it was me on the phone. "Just gross!"

So much for not getting emotional. For the next ten minutes Sara explained just why she thought Ted was gross. She said he was conceited, boring, and octopus-handed.

"At least *Paul's* good looks haven't gone to his head?" she informed me.

Soon I realized that her sour mood would not bring out much good advice. For the rest of the conversation she talked about how great Paul was and how going out with Ted made her want to ask Paul out more than ever. On Monday, she said, she'd do it.

I was overwhelmed. What could I say to her? What more could I do to talk her out of her plan? I knew I should simply tell her the truth—that I'd seen Marci flirting with Paul and he had seemed very interested in her. But I couldn't. I didn't want to be the one to hurt her. Maybe, I hoped, Paul would let her down easy.

I laced up my sneaker, wishing it were black. Even brown would be better. Any dark color would do. Everything I was wearing would blend into the night well—the black turtleneck sweater that had been part of my Halloween costume two years before—I was disgusted that it still fit—a pair of black corduroy jeans, and brown socks. My powder blue jogging shoes didn't exactly match the rest of my outfit, but at least I could run in them if I had to.

The thought of having to run away from something made me shiver. It also reminded me of the seriousness of my plan. Right after talking to Sara, I had decided on a course of action. Maybe I couldn't save *her* from heartbreak, but I could still help Marion. If Burke was deceiving her, I would find out.

Pulling on my mom's navy blue Windbreaker, I thanked my lucky stars that she and my dad had gone to a friend's house for dinner. All they knew was that I'd be out with friends at a party for the evening. It wasn't exactly the whole truth, but it was close enough that I didn't feel too guilty. Jake, thank goodness, was also at a friend's house watching movies on his friend's VCR, which would keep him busy for ages. At least I didn't have to worry about running into him in my spy clothes.

As I locked the front door behind me, I felt a little stab of regret over the fun I'd be missing that night. Greg had asked me to a movie. Of course, he probably would have wanted to see *Godzilla Takes Chicago* or something, but even that would have been OK. We never actually *watched* most of the movies we went to, anyway. We were always too busy laughing and kissing and holding hands and fighting over the popcorn.

I thought of Greg all the way down Sierra to the bus stop. When he asked me to go to the movies with him, I'd said I wasn't feeling well. Instead, I'd be sneaking around in a ridiculous outfit, praying that no one would recognize me.

On the bus I checked to see if I had everything. In my pockets I had a map, some spare change, and Anne Bainbridge's address, which I had scribbled on a tiny piece of paper. She lived at 691 Winslow Drive, all the way out in West Oaks. I knew that neighborhood about as well as I knew Singapore. The town map gave me a pretty good idea of how to get there, but still I felt lost, even before I got off the bus.

And things continued to get worse.

The streets all ran the way they were supposed to, so that part was easy. I made a left on West Oaks Road, then a right three blocks up on Winslow. But the huge, expensive houses and sprawling front lawns gave me the creeps. For one thing, whoever planned the neighborhood had not believed in sidewalks, so I had to walk on the edge of the road. And everything was so empty and quiet—not a bit like our neighborhood. Where I lived, the small houses hugged the street on bicycle-littered lawns, and voices drifted out from winking windows. In West Oaks, each house stood alone like a castle.

Suddenly a cool breeze stirred, and a dry leaf whispered across the pavement behind me. I jumped. There was no one around, and not even a tree for a person to hide behind. But a spooky feeling engulfed me, anyway, as if I were being watched.

The thought sent a chill up my spine. I shivered, took a deep breath, and kept walking.

Anne's house turned out to be pretty easy to find. Cars lined the street in front of it. Lights blazed in practically every room. And as I drew closer, I heard rock music pouring through the open windows. The music part, I didn't mind. In fact, I welcomed it. A little music could go a long way toward muffling a spy's footsteps. But the light I could have done without. It spilled out in wide pools on the grass outside each window, leaving few shadows in which to hide.

First I scanned the rows of cars. If Burke's wasn't there, maybe he hadn't come after all. My heart sank as I spotted the old green Toyota.

I hid behind a tree at the edge of the lawn, going over my strategy. A hundred times already that day I had wondered if I should just go into Anne's party. Of course, I hadn't been invited, but maybe no one would notice. From the noise and the number of cars, there seemed to be at least fifty people inside. Who would notice little, unimportant me?

Burke. He would notice me, and that was the problem. If he happened to see me, one of Marion's best friends, he'd be on his best behavior from then on. He would just let his inspection of the "fox" wait for another time.

Tonight, I told myself, *you've got to settle this question, one way or the other.*

I decided to stay outside. Like something out of a cartoon, I raced across the lawn to another tree on the side of the house. From there, though, all I could see were shapes of people moving around inside. Who they were, and whether any of them happened to be Burke flirting with another girl, I couldn't tell. I took a quick look around to make sure the coast was clear, then dashed toward the nearest window.

Please, I prayed to the patron saints and gods of worthy spies. *Don't let the neighbors see. And please don't let anyone mistake me for someone they should call the police about.*

My heart pounded so hard that I could barely breathe. For a moment I crouched nervously under the window ledge. Fortunately the window was closed. It would be hard for anyone to hear me over the music.

Peeking around the edge of the redwood planter box on the ledge, I struggled to see into the house. The petunias in the box blocked my view, as did the huge armchair inside. I grabbed onto the ledge and pulled myself up so just the tips of my toes were touching the ground. My nose brushed a petunia petal as I leaned closer.

Then I heard a muffled snap, like the sound of a twig breaking. As I whirled around, a dozen possibilities raced through my mind. It was the police SWAT team, called out by a cautious neighbor. Or maybe the Bainbridges had a trained attack dog, who bit before he barked. Those fears gave way instantly to a different kind of alarm when I saw who it was.

Chapter Eleven

The very last person I expected to see was the one I turned around to face.

"Greg?" I whispered in shock.

His eyes blazed in the dim light.

I reached for his hand, but he pulled it away.

"Why didn't you just tell me the truth, Allie?"

My head spun. I felt like I was trapped in a bad dream. I opened my mouth to answer, but nothing would come out.

"If you wanted to chase after some other guy," he said in a low, even voice, "you should have just told me."

His mouth was set in a hard line as if he were struggling to keep from yelling at me. Everything about him, from the way his fists were jammed into his jacket pockets to the stiffness in his shoulders, told me how angry he was.

"But I don't *want* to chase any other guy," I said. "There *is* no one else."

"Then what are you doing out here?"

"Greg, it's not how it looks—" I said quickly.

"Oh? How do you think it looks?" he countered. "All I know, Allie, is that for a long time you've been hiding something from me. Tonight I asked you to go out with me, and you said you were sick. Then on my way to the movies, I saw you ride by on a bus. What was I supposed to think? Should I just have ignored it?"

The bus, I thought as everything became clear to me. "You mean you followed me here?" I asked in disbelief.

"Yes." He nodded. "I did."

For a moment all I could do was stare at him. Greg had been following me! A little prickle of indignation rose up inside me. In seconds it had grown into full-fledged anger. How dare he do this to me! Didn't he trust me? The very thought of Greg sneaking around after me, spying on my every move—

Then my thoughts came to a screeching halt. Sneaking, spying, mistrusting—what, exactly, had *I* been doing all these weeks?

I leaned against the wall of the house for support.

"I'm sorry," I whispered.

Greg straightened up as if I had slapped him. "So you *were* waiting for someone out here."

"No, Greg. I wasn't. I—" The words froze in my throat. How could I tell him what I'd been doing? I felt so ashamed of my spying, just like the kid who makes fun of a fat classmate until the teacher comes and explains how mean that is.

He sighed. His shoulders relaxed, and the look in his eyes was no longer fiery, but flat. "I shouldn't be interrogating you," he muttered tonelessly. Then he gave me a long, searching look and turned and walked away.

For a second I couldn't move—I was too shocked. But then I recovered and ran across the lawn after him. I couldn't have cared less who saw me. What was important was that Greg was walking away from me and he was hurt.

"Greg, please. Wait."

He looked over his shoulder at me but didn't stop walking.

"Greg, listen. I wasn't waiting for anyone. Really! I mean, why would I have been meeting them out here in the dark?"

"You didn't want anyone to see you with someone else. So you arranged to meet him outside." He walked faster.

My mouth hung open a little. What a nasty thing to say! How could he think I would do such a horrible thing? Then I remembered the things he had said a few weeks before. "I was pretty possessive, I guess, maybe it was because I'm an only child . . . I've never had a girlfriend before." He had been trying to share his feelings with me, trying to let me know how much he cared about me. Perhaps, right then, he was mean because he cared so much.

"Greg," I began softly, "I would never do something like that. I would never see anyone behind your back. I wouldn't do that to anyone I cared about. Especially"—my voice quavered a little—"not to you."

We had reached his car. He just stared at the door. Then he turned back to face me.

"Is that really true, Allie?" His face was still set in a rigid expression.

"Yes, really. I—I wouldn't hurt you for the world."

He gave me a searching look, as if he could see clear through me if he tried hard enough. Then he sighed. "I'm sorry. I really have no right to question you like this."

"Oh, Greg, but you do have a right. I mean, you deserve an explanation."

He shifted his weight and crossed his arms. "Well, if you weren't meeting someone here, why are you dressed like that? You've never dressed that sexy for a date with me."

My eyes flew to my spy suit.

"All that black," he said. "And that tight sweater."

"This?" I asked, tugging on my old turtleneck. I couldn't help laughing. "You call *this* sexy?" The thought of my old cat costume being sexy was just too much. My laughter stopped abruptly when I noticed his expression. He was not amused.

"Oh, Greg, I'm sorry. I mean, this wasn't supposed to look"— I giggled again— "sexy."

"Well, then? How was it supposed to look?"

He was frowning again, and I didn't want to make him any angrier. I tried to control myself, which turned out to be pretty easy once I realized the time had come to provide reasons for my strange behavior. What on earth would I say? How could I ever explain why I'd been sneaking around the Bainbridges' house, peeking in at the windows?

I looked at him, took a deep breath, and started by saying, "You're never going to believe this."

The lights on Shepherd Avenue are beautiful at night. They cast a soft golden glow over the sidewalk and darkened storefronts. A few years ago the observatory up on Mt. Monk asked the valley towns to put in the new, softer kind of light to keep the sky dark for star watching.

As we drove along, I concentrated on those lights and the empty shops, trying to stay calm. Greg gripped the steering wheel with both hands and stared straight ahead.

"You've got to be joking," he finally whispered. "Mission: *Love*?"

"Yes," I answered, almost inaudibly.

His mouth twisted into a frown. "You mean you girls actually went around *spying* on people?"

I bit my lip. "That was the basic idea."

Slowly he shook his head. "Oh, man!"

I sank down into the seat, wishing I could crawl under it and hide. What must Greg think of me now? Maybe I shouldn't have explained to him about the mission. Maybe it would have been better if I had let him believe that I'd been meeting another guy at Anne's party. At least that would seem a lot more normal!

"Spying," he repeated, eyes still on the road. "I never would have dreamed—"

My thumbnail was nearly in shreds. I wanted to cry out to Greg, to convince him that I really wasn't as mean and/or crazy as he was probably thinking I was. But I didn't say a word. It seemed I had already said enough.

"I guess," Greg said, "that I don't need to ask who came up with this scheme."

That's right, I thought. *You don't need to ask.*

But he did anyway. "It was you, right?"

I nodded. Then I stared out the window, afraid to look at him. I didn't want to see the expression on his face. It would reflect all the terrible things he was thinking about me. And the worst part was, he had a right to think them. Only that night had I realized how unfair spying was. A couple of days before, I had been willing to give up Mission: Love because it seemed dangerous and childish, but that night the tables had been turned. Greg's spying on me had made me mad. And even worse, it had hurt me. I was hurt because he hadn't trusted me. Wouldn't Burke, Paul, Bob, Dennis, and our other targets have felt the same way? At the very least, they wouldn't appreciate having their privacy invaded. For the first time, I had been put in the target's place. And I hadn't liked it one bit.

I looked at Greg, about to explain and apologize. I would say that I should have considered other people's feelings. I should have considered *his* feelings, too.

But he was smiling. Then, as he returned my gaze, the smile grew. Before I had time to think, he was laughing.

"What's so funny?" I asked, by then completely bewildered.

He pulled off to the side of the road and put the car in park.

"Oh, Allie," he said quietly.

"I guess you don't believe me, do you?" I asked solemnly.

He shook his head. "I do, honest. It's just—so funny." He laughed again. "I mean, I bet you were spying that time you got caught under the library table, weren't you?"

I nodded. "Yes, I was. You do believe me, then?"

"I guess it's too crazy a story not to believe."

"And you're not mad?" I asked.

He paused, tapping the steering wheel with his thumbs. "Well, I don't know. Did you ever spy on me?"

I looked at my hands and winced. "Once."

"You did? When?"

I told him all about the night Sara and I had trailed him. "But I felt really terrible about it," I explained. "I mean, I hated snooping on you that way, but since it ended up bringing us together, I—"

"Oh, wow," he interrupted. "You sneak. We never suspected a thing! You deserve—you deserve a good tickling for this."

I squealed when he leaned across the seat and went for my ribs. But then I poked a finger into his side, too. In a minute we were both weak from laughing, and we fell into each other's arms.

After we recovered, Greg cupped my chin in his palm, lifting it gently. "I guess you're right about your spying bringing us together. That was the night I realized how much I liked you."

"It was?"

He nodded. "What's that old saying? 'All's well that ends well'?"

I nodded and slipped my fingers into the rich mane of curls at the nape of his neck. Greg lowered his lips to mine and touched them with a long, lingering kiss.

I sighed. "That's a good saying."

Then we realized that the engine was still running. Greg took my hand and held it tenderly as we set off for my house.

We were turning up Sierra Street when he spoke again. "This spying business explains a lot of things to me, Allie."

"It does? Like what?"

"Oh, like the strange way you've acted at times. As I said, I knew you were hiding something from me."

"You did? How?"

"Well, the first time I got suspicious was after that first movie we saw together. You went in the restroom and stayed in there forever. Then, when I finally found you, you acted really spaced out and distracted. It was as if you couldn't have cared less about being with me."

"Oh, Greg. I really did care, but—"

"Yeah, let me guess. You saw some guy you had to spy on for Nicky."

I had to smile. "Pretty close. He was for Sara."

Greg grinned back. "See, I've got it figured now. There was another time, too. After that library thing, remember how you wouldn't talk to me about it?"

"That was a terrible day," I muttered.

"I could tell you were more than just embarrassed. And then there were all the times when you and your friends would stop talking the second I walked up. You'd be talking away, and then as soon as I came within earshot, you'd stop and look guilty. It didn't seem like ordinary girl talk to me."

I looked at him out of the corner of my eye. "You know," I observed, "you, Mr. Segura, would make a pretty good spy yourself."

"Oh, yeah?"

"Definitely," I said. "And you did a pretty good job of trailing me tonight. We should have—hey, what a great idea. We should have recruited *you* for the mission! You could have gone into the guys' locker room and everything!"

He gave a long sigh and rolled his eyes. "Boy, I really missed out, didn't I?"

As we pulled up in front of my house, I gazed at his profile. It was so fine, almost delicate. Sensitive, I thought. That's what it was. And that's what Greg was, too. He certainly did act different from other guys. Most boys I knew wouldn't have picked up on half of what Greg had sensed right away. I couldn't imagine John or Kevin noticing that I was distracted on a date. But Greg—Greg cared about me. He had tried to tell me so, too. He'd tried to say something that afternoon we went walking in the park, but I had been so wrapped up in Mission: Love and my friends' problems that I hadn't really listened to him. I had shut him out instead. And I'd almost lost him, too.

"Greg," I said softly. "I want to tell you—" I paused and looked down. "I'm sorry."

He didn't answer, squeezing my hand instead.

"All that time while I was acting suspicious and giving you reason to doubt me, I never—I never realized how you might feel. I was too busy worrying about my friends."

Gently he held a finger to my lips. "I just have one question," he said.

"What?"

"Is it over?" He lifted one eyebrow.

"Mission: Love?" I nodded. "Over and out."

"That," he murmured, "is all I wanted to know."

He took me in his arms and held me tightly for a long, long time.

Chapter Twelve

I opened my eyes on Sunday morning and blinked against the sun pouring in through the opening in the curtains. A bird was singing outside my window. Every note came through separate and clear, as if the bird were practicing a piece slowly, the way Sara sometimes does on her flute.

Good morning, Allie, I imagined it was singing. *This is the start of a gorgeous day. Come look.*

When I opened the curtains all the way, I found a world washed in blues and greens and golds. Tingles swept through me.

"Good morning!" I called back to the bird and hopped out of bed.

All the way to the kitchen I hummed.

Jake frowned at me from the breakfast

table. "Do you have to make that noise? You sound like a mosquito." Jake is not known for his early-morning cheer.

I simply smiled at him, still humming, then went over to give my mother a kiss. From behind her teacup, she flashed me one of her knowing grins. She knew why I was feeling so happy.

One of these days, I figured, I'd fill her in on some of the details. But just then, I wanted to keep my sweet, contented feeling to myself. It was as if the whole world were fresh and new. Not only because of my talk with Greg the night before, but also because of Mission: Love. Or rather, because Mission: Love was over. I felt as if a huge weight had been lifted from my shoulders.

Why, exactly, I felt so relieved didn't really come clear to me until Sara called that afternoon.

Her first words poured out in a flood. "Oh, Allie, it's so incredible—I asked Paul out, then he asked me and we went to a party—"

"Whoa!" I interrupted. "Did you say you went out with Paul?"

She sighed. "Yes. Yes!"

Her news took a moment to digest. "You said you asked him first?"

"Well, I did, but then he said he had been wanting to ask me out but was afraid to, so—"

"What?" I had never, but never, heard her so excited before. "Sara, please, slow down a little."

She sighed again. "All right. But, Allie, it was just so—*wonderful*."

Her voice sounded soft and dreamy. Gone were Sara's usual, measured words.

"What happened," she explained, "was that I walked right up to Paul and asked him if he wanted to see the new exhibit at the science museum with me on Sunday. You should have seen me, Allie. My voice didn't shake at all. Then he said he'd really like to, but couldn't because his grandfather would be visiting. At that point I thought I'd just shrivel up. But then he asked me if I'd like to go with him to Anne Bainbridge's party."

I bolted upright. "Anne Bainbridge's party?"

"Yes, last night."

"Did you go?" I demanded.

"Oh, yes. I did."

My reactions were a jumble. I didn't know which to deal with first.

"And do you know what he said?" Sara went on.

"What?"

"That he had been wanting to ask me out for weeks. *Weeks*, Allie. Imagine! He said I usually acted so serious around him that he thought I didn't like him, and that's why he didn't ask me before."

At that point there was no question as to which emotion would take first place. I felt like a mean, meddling old fool. Thanks to my butting in, Sara had almost missed out on the chance to go out with Paul! I had come just inches away from ruining things for her.

"Well, isn't it terrific?" she asked.

I brought myself back to the matter at hand. "Oh, yes, Sara. It's fantastic!"

From there she launched into a fond description of Paul's incredible green eyes and an account of his asking her out to dinner the following week. I could only half listen. My mind spun with the realization of how much damage our spying could have caused. Sure, it had been fun for a while—all the secret plans and whispers. But the problem was that we had ended up taking it too seriously. We had hinged some pretty important decisions on information that wasn't always right. Just because Paul had flirted a little with Marci, for instance, didn't mean he wanted to go out with her.

"We danced practically all night at the party," Sara continued.

With that, another question came to mind. If Sara had been at Anne's party, maybe she had seen the "fox." *No,* I told myself firmly. *Whether or not Sara saw Burke there is none of my business. I mustn't start thinking like a spy again.*

Sara began telling me about how crowded the party had been with the jock crowd and how Paul had been invited only because he often helped a couple of the football players with math.

"Do you want to hear something really sad?" she asked suddenly.

I was about to say no, not particularly, when she went on.

"Burke," she said.

"Burke?" I repeated. "He was there?"

"Well," Sara replied. "In a way."

My stomach turned over. I couldn't stand the suspense.

"All night," she said. "Burke did not budge from the backgammon board. He had a game going with some friend of his the whole time. And he had the saddest look on his face, Allie. Everybody kept trying to get him to dance, but he wouldn't. He just sat there and moped over Marion's being gone for the weekend."

"He did?" I was so relieved I practically sang the words.

"I heard someone say that whenever she's gone, he gets this way."

I had to laugh. Sara made it sound as if that were a crime.

After we hung up, I just sat for a while thinking things over. I still had no clue about who the girl Burke and his friends had been talking about was, but I guessed it didn't matter any longer. Maybe I never would get over my urge to meddle and snoop. Maybe being the baby in the family had helped make me that way. But I felt pretty sure that Mission: Love had taught me a lesson. My friends, at least, could get along perfectly well without my spying for them. In fact, it seemed they were better off without my snooping around.

As I mentioned earlier, time has a way of whizzing by when you're enjoying yourself. That's exactly what happened to me that spring semester, mostly because of Greg and the fun we had together. As a result I didn't see the gang as much anymore. Or, at least, it seemed as though I hardly ever saw them because I was used to spending at least four or five afternoons or evenings a week with them. Now I only saw them for about two.

So, when we all went to the spring class picnic together, I was excited. Boyfriends would be allowed, but only as an afterthought. This was to be a girls' day out.

Nicky brought her giant purple and yellow beach blanket and spread it over a soft, shady patch of grass.

"This is really wonderful," Marion murmured as we all sprawled out on the blanket.

"Surely you're not referring to that lunch they just served us." Sara scrunched up her nose. "I didn't think there was a way to ruin hot dogs and potato salad.".

"They found a way," Nicky mumbled as she chewed a blade of grass. Her feet were propped against a tree, right next to my head.

"I was referring," said Marion, "to this." She made a broad, sweeping gesture with one of her graceful hands. "The flowers, the sky—"

"The absence of bothersome boys," Nicky added.

"Bothersome?" Sara repeated.

"Well, I mean it's nice to have it be just us girls for a while, isn't it?"

Sara nodded. I glanced down the hill at the playing field. A coed softball game was in progress, and the cheers and yells were muffled a bit, but still audible.

A butterfly fluttered in the silence nearby.

That, combined with the sweet May heat, made me feel deliciously lazy.

"It amazes me, though," Sara said, "that the Nicky Gould fan club has left us alone for this long."

Nicky shrugged. Then she rolled over on her stomach, barely missing my head with the swing of her feet. "I'm cutting back," she announced.

Marion lifted an eyebrow. "On boys?"

"Mmm-hmm. I'm whittling it down. These days I'm dating just the boys I really like."

"Oh," Sara nodded. "You mean Ben Lee and Dennis Conroy and Bob Lopez and Joel Saks and Ron Ellis and—"

We all cracked up.

"Oh, cut it out," Nicky snapped, giving Sara a nudge with her foot.

I yawned. "What brought this on, Nicky?"

She frowned thoughtfully and plucked a blade of grass. "I guess I got to thinking about it because of Mission: Love."

I stopped yawning. "You did?"

"Yup." She nodded. "I figured that if I had to go around spying on the boys I know to find out what they thought about me, then they must not be very good friends. I mean, I was going out with a lot of guys I didn't really feel comfortable with, you know?"

We all nodded with understanding, even though none of us had ever had that particular problem. Nicky was the only one of us with a surplus of guys around.

"Well," Marion said, "I suppose I was wrong."

"About what?" asked Nicky.

"The cloak and dagger project. It wasn't such a horrible idea, really. Somehow, it managed to do us each some good."

"Yeah," Nicky agreed. "I kind of miss it."

I, for one, did not miss it. But I wasn't about to say so. Mission: Love had, after all, been my idea.

"Look." Sara suddenly sat forward. "The game's over."

Gazing down the little hill, I picked out Greg's curly auburn head right away. Watching the way he walked, with that agile spring, filled me with pride.

A little while later everyone ran off to get watermelon. But Greg, collapsing on the blanket beside me, held me back for a moment.

"What have your friends been plotting while we were gone?" he asked. "Another mission?"

"Maybe." I grinned, tracing his cheekbone with my finger. "And maybe I'm on a mission right this very moment."

"Are you?" His deep brown eyes glinted in the sun.

I nodded. "It's the best one yet. And you're even helping me."

At first his eyebrows came together in a confused expression, but before long he began to smile. In his eyes, the light danced.

"Oh," he said. "I get it." He bent his head for a kiss, and then he whispered, "You and me. It's the new, improved Mission: Love."